"You know what?" Alanna interrupted. "Forget it. You're right. I'll be fine. I just need to get over it and let it go. Thanks. I'll talk to you later," she added, and before Conner could respond, she pressed the off button on her cordless phone and threw the receiver down on her bed.

The problem was she wasn't going to just get over it. She was still reeling from all the things her father had said to her, and now she was fuming about Conner's insensitivity, too. Alanna picked up the phone again. If only she could find someone who would just listen and sympathize without telling her what she was doing wrong. But who? She stared at the numbers on the phone face and tried to think of someone she could call.

Don't miss any of the books in SWEET VALLEY HIGH
SENIOR YEAR, an exciting series from Bantam Books!

Visit the Official Sweet Valley Web Site on the Internet at:

www.sweetvalley.com

Francine Pascal's SVH senioryear

Touch and Go

CREATED BY
FRANCINE PASCAL

BANTAM BOOKS
NEW YORK·TORONTO·LONDON·SYDNEY·AUCKLAND

RL: 6, AGES 012 AND UP

TOUCH AND GO
A Bantam Book / June 2002

Sweet Valley High® is a registered trademark of Francine Pascal.
Conceived by Francine Pascal.
Cover photography by Michael Segal.

Copyright © 2002 by Francine Pascal.
Cover copyright © 2002 by 17th Street Productions,
an Alloy, Inc. company.

Produced by 17th Street Productions,
an Alloy, Inc. company.
151 West 26th Street
New York, NY 10011.

ISBN: 0-553-49391-4

Visit us on the Web! www.randomhouse.com/teens

Published simultaneously in the United States and Canada

Bantam Books is an imprint of Random House Children's Books, a
division of Random House, Inc. BANTAM BOOKS and the rooster
colophon are registered trademarks of Random House, Inc. Bantam Books,
1540 Broadway, New York, New York 10036.

PRINTED IN THE UNITED STATES OF AMERICA

OPM   0 9 8 7 6 5 4 3 2 1

To Ben Markowitz

Love 101: Is Your Guy Mr. Right?

Question 4

When it comes to trust and loyalty, my guy is most like a:

(a) **Saint Bernard.** He's big, strong, and cuddly, and I can always count on him.

(b) **Husky.** He's fierce and protective, but he'll warm up to someone new if the approach is right.

(c) **Wild dog.** When he's off the leash, he's out of control.

Andy Marsden

Saint Bernard? Husky? Wild dog? You've got to be kidding. Why do I let Tia talk me into taking these stupid quizzes?

Oh, all right. If I had to choose one, I guess it would be (a), a Saint Bernard. Not that Dave's exactly cuddly. And he doesn't drool like a Saint Bernard either—at least not that I've noticed. But I do trust him. And I think he'd be there for me even if things got tough.

I mean, look what he's done already. He came out to his dad, and he's actually being pretty open about our relationship.

That's just not the kind of stuff you'd expect from a husky. Or a wild dog.

Alanna Feldman

(b) Husky.

Sure, Conner seemed loyal and trustworthy at first. But the second I was out of the picture, what did he do? He hooked up with Elizabeth Wakefield again. In a matter of days! How lame is that?

I can't believe I actually trusted him. Yeah, he was fierce and protective for a while, but he definitely warmed up to Elizabeth. And now I'm out in the cold.

melissa Fox

(c) wild dog.
He cheated on me with Jessica Wakefield, and he cheated on me with Erika Brooks. But Will Simmons is about to get a little of his own back, and I can't wait to see the look on his "wild dog" face when he does.

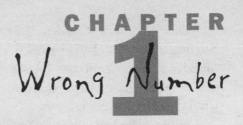

Wrong Number

"Hello, you've reached the Feldman residence," came Mrs. Feldman's syrupy voice. "Jake, Joanna, and Alanna can't come to the phone right now, but if you leave a message, we'll get back to you as soon as possible. Have a lovely day."

As soon as he heard the beep, Conner began speaking. "Alanna, this is Conner. I—" He stopped short. "Hello?" For some reason, the answering machine had cut him off. He sighed and punched in Alanna's number again, then waited for the beep.

"Hey, Alanna," he started, but once again he heard a click and then a dial tone. "That's weird," he muttered, checking his grip on the phone to make sure he hadn't inadvertently hung up on himself. It didn't look like he had done anything, but just to make sure, Conner turned off the phone, gave it a minute, then turned it on again and waited for a fresh dial tone. Then he carefully punched in Alanna's number for the third time.

"Alanna, this is Conner. Your machine keeps hanging up on—" Conner paused. For a moment it sounded like someone had picked up on the other end. "Hello? Alanna?" he called, but it was silent. Until the dial tone cut in.

Conner clenched his jaw. "Stupid machine," he muttered. All he wanted to do was leave one simple message. Was that too much to ask? *Apparently, yes.* He set the phone on his desk, reclined in his chair, and clasped his hands behind his head.

Maybe he should just send Alanna a quick e-mail instead. At least her computer couldn't cut him off halfway through the message. Conner pulled out the keyboard tray at the center of his desk and hit the power button to start up his Mac, but as soon as he'd done it, he knew it was a bad idea. Alanna wasn't always good about checking her e-mail, and judging by the way she'd run off before, he knew the message that there was nothing between him and Elizabeth was one she needed to get sooner rather than later. Which meant he needed to try one more time.

Reluctantly Conner grasped the receiver and punched in Alanna's number. *But this is it,* he told himself. If he got cut off again, he was just going to forget about it. Alanna would realize he'd tried to leave a message, and she'd just have to call him back.

"Hey—your machine is whacked," he started in

at the beep, "so I'm going to make this quick. I'm not interested in Elizabeth Wakefield. She—"

"Did you say Elizabeth Wakefield?" a voice interrupted. "I'm sorry. You must have the wrong number. Elizabeth Wakefield doesn't live here."

"Alanna?" Conner said, but it was too late. She had already hung up. *Great,* he thought. So she'd been right there, listening to him the whole time. And hanging up on him. Which meant the answering machine was fine. Alanna, on the other hand, clearly was not.

He picked up the phone again and punched in seven more digits.

"*Buenas noches,* Ramirez residence."

"Can't you just say hello?" he grumbled.

Tia laughed. "Someone's in a good mood," she teased. "What's up?"

"Alanna's pissed at me."

There was a brief silence. "Um . . . I don't want to sound harsh or anything," Tia began, "but . . . isn't that kind of *old* news?"

"It was. But she stopped by tonight."

"Oh," Tia said. "What for?"

"To talk, I think. But Liz was here."

"Oops."

"Yeah. Alanna flipped out."

"Well, what were you and Liz *doing?*" Tia asked.

3

"Working on some stuff for Quigley's class."

"And did you explain that to Alanna?"

"I didn't get a chance. She took off, and now she won't even answer the phone. She just keeps hanging up on me."

"Hold on. Did you say *keeps* hanging up on you?" Tia asked. "As in, more than once?"

Conner clenched his jaw. "I thought it was the answering machine," he said.

"But it wasn't?"

"No," Conner answered. He stood up and rubbed the back of his neck with his free hand. "It was Alanna."

"Hanging up on you? Repeatedly?" Tia asked. Conner could practically hear her eyes popping out of their sockets.

He walked over to his bed and sat down on the edge. "Yes."

"Wow," Tia said. "I just can't picture you . . . you know . . . calling back. *Over* and *over* again."

Conner felt his hand tightening on the receiver and forced himself to relax it. "Whatever," he said. "So what should I do?"

There was a pause. "Wait a second," Tia said. "You're calling *me* to find out what to do?"

Conner rolled his eyes. "Yeah. So?"

"It's just that . . . well, I don't think you've ever asked for my advice before," Tia said. "I mean, I've given it to you plenty of times, but I'm pretty sure this is the first time you've actually asked for it. Are you feeling okay?"

"I'm fine," Conner said.

"And you want my advice?" Tia said, the grin evident in her tone.

"Well," Conner said, "you *are* a girl."

"Whoa," Tia exclaimed. "I'm a *girl?* What's that supposed to mean?"

"It means you probably have a better idea what's going on inside Alanna's head than I do."

"Why? Because I'm a girl?"

"Yeah," Conner said with a shrug. Was it really that difficult a concept to grasp?

"That is so sexist," Tia protested. "You know, just because your ex-girlfriend and I share a gender, it doesn't mean we think alike—because we don't. *At all.* In fact, aside from being female, I doubt the two of us have a single thing in common."

"Jeez, dial it back, Tee. I just figured you might know what she wants because you're insightful."

"Yeah. I know," Tia said.

"So?" he asked. "Any ideas?"

"Well," she said finally. "If it were me, I guess I'd want some kind of assurance from you and Liz that there was nothing going on."

"From me *and* Liz?" Conner asked.

5

"Uh-huh. Because if you got Liz to come talk to me about everything, then I'd know *I* was the one you wanted."

Conner narrowed his eyes. "What? That doesn't make sense."

"Yes, it does," Tia replied. "Because by getting Liz to tell me there's nothing going on, you'd be making it clear to her too. See?"

"Yeah, I see," Conner said, "but it's stupid. And it's impossible too. There's no way I'm asking my ex-ex-girlfriend to explain things to my current ex."

"Then I guess you're stuck," Tia said. "Bye, now."

"Wait!" Conner yelled. "Come on, Tee—isn't there something else I could do?"

"You could try calling again," Tia suggested.

"Yeah, right. And if I get tired of hearing the dial tone, I could just go over and let her slam the door in my face for a while."

"Sure. And if you get tired of that, you could come over here and let *me* slam the door on you a few times. It could be fun."

Conner groaned. "All right. Fine. I'm sorry for the girl comment. Now will you help me?"

"I would, Conner, but I don't know what else to do. I gave you my suggestion, and you didn't like it."

"Well, maybe *you* could talk to her," Conner suggested. "You know—instead of Liz."

"No way!" Tia said. "This is your relationship—not mine."

"Come on, Tee. You said yourself she'd believe it more if I got someone else to tell her too."

"I said you should get *Liz* to talk to her," Tia replied. "Not me."

"But she'd listen to you," Conner insisted.

"Why—because I'm a girl?"

Well, yeah, Conner thought, but he wasn't about to make the same mistake twice. "No, because . . . you're better at this stuff than I am," he said, marveling at how good it sounded.

"Uh-uh. No way. I'm not going over there," Tia said. "This is your thing, and you need to do it."

"Oh, right. Like I've never bailed you out before," Conner said. Guilt seemed the next logical step.

"Actually," Tia said, "I don't think you ever have."

"Of course I have," Conner said. "What about that time in second grade when Brad Nelson was picking on you, and I—"

"He was picking on *Andy,*" Tia interrupted, "and I punched him. You just sat at the top of the slide and laughed."

"Oh. Right," Conner said. Why did Tia always have to remember that stuff so clearly? "Still—I'm sure I've helped you out before. Can't you just go over to Alanna's and tell her I'm not with Liz?"

7

"Why can't you do it yourself?" Tia asked.

"Because she won't talk to me," Conner reminded her. "And besides, I'm sick of all these head trips."

"It's called *dating*, Conner," Tia said.

"Whatever. Can you just fix this for me? You know, take care of all the drama?"

"I don't know. . . . I—"

"Just this one time," Conner said. "I'll owe you one."

"You owe me about two billion already," Tia said.

"So what's two billion and one?"

Tia moaned, and Conner knew he had her. "Fine," she said. "I'll talk to her tomorrow. But you're taking me to the Gazebo for ice cream this week."

"Sure," Conner replied.

"And I don't just mean a plain cone, single-scoop thing. I'm talking the Fudge Brownie Deluxe Sundae with as many toppings as I want."

"Absolutely," Conner agreed, knowing that if Tia could actually fix things between him and Alanna, he'd be willing to buy her three. Or even four. Whatever she wanted. After all, a dish of ice cream—even if it was a really big one—was a small price to pay for getting rid of a relationship headache. And, unlike involving Elizabeth or having Alanna slam the door in his face twenty-two times, it was a price he was willing to pay.

*   *   *

Today the part of the meddling friend will be played by Tia Ramirez, Tia thought as she walked up the brick pathway to Alanna's house. She stood in front of the red wooden door, staring at the brass door knocker and wondering what on earth she had been thinking when she'd agreed to this.

Why am I here again? she asked herself. *Oh, that's right. To patch things up between my best friend and his unreliable, neurotic girlfriend.* What a trip. For a moment she contemplated turning around and going home, but she'd told Conner she'd help him, and Tia wasn't one to go back on her word.

Reluctantly she pressed the doorbell, wondering why the Feldmans needed a door knocker *and* a bell, but her thought was cut short.

"Tia?" Alanna said, eyeing her from head to toe. "What are you doing here?"

"Meddling," Tia muttered, staring down at her clogs.

"What?"

"Nothing," Tia said, meeting Alanna's gaze. "I'm just . . . Conner wanted me to come talk to you and let you know that there's nothing going on between him and Liz."

"If Conner wants to tell me something, he can tell me himself," Alanna huffed. She stepped back from the door and started to swing it closed, but Tia stopped it with her hand.

9

"Well, maybe if you'd stop hanging up on him, he would," Tia said.

Alanna folded her arms across her chest. "Is that all?" she asked. "Or was there something else he wanted you to tell me?"

Sheesh, Tia thought, *what does Conner see in her anyway?* From Tia's perspective, Alanna had brought him nothing but grief—and now she was giving it to Tia too.

"Look—you don't have to get hostile. I'm only here because you keep shutting Conner out. If you'd just give him a chance, he'd tell you all this stuff himself, but I don't know what you can expect when you won't even talk to him."

Alanna blinked and shifted her gaze so that she was looking just over Tia's left shoulder instead of straight into her eyes. "So he told you that I hung up on him?" she asked.

"Mm-hmm. And that you ran off last night when you saw Liz," Tia said.

"Wouldn't you?" Alanna asked. "I mean, if your boyfriend was hanging out with his ex without telling you?"

"And just when was he supposed to tell you?" Tia asked. "You weren't talking to him, Alanna. In fact, you told him you never wanted to see him again, didn't you?"

"Yeah, but—" Alanna brought one hand to her face and rubbed her forehead. "I don't know," she said, her voice cracking. "I'm just so confused."

"About what?" Tia said, surprising herself with the brashness of her voice. What did she have to be so indignant about? This was between Conner and Alanna. It had nothing to do with her. Except, of course, that Conner was counting on her to fix everything.

"About Conner," Alanna said. "I mean, Liz was his first serious girlfriend, right?" Tia nodded. "So why was he hanging out with her if not because . . ." Her voice trailed off, but Tia knew where she was headed.

"Because they both write," Tia said. "And they both get all hyped up about it. That's all. Really. They were working on some assignment for their creative writing class."

"But . . . why does he have to work with *her*? Isn't there someone else in his class he can study with?"

"I don't know," Tia said. "You'd have to ask him—but that's my point. You're going to have to actually *talk* to him if you want to get any of this straightened out."

"I guess," Alanna said with a sigh, but Tia could tell she wasn't exactly ready to charge to the phone and call him. *All right,* she thought, taking a deep

11

breath. *This is for you, Conner. And for my sundae.*

"Look. I know you got all freaked out when Conner showed up in Chicago with your parents. And I can understand that you might have felt a little betrayed. But did you ever stop to think how hard it must have been for Conner to even approach your parents, knowing how much they hated him? I mean, they practically accused him of kidnapping you when they first realized you were gone. But still, he tracked you down and came over here and talked to them, and he convinced them to let *him* come get you, knowing the whole time how angry you were going to be when you found out your parents were there too. Did you ever wonder why he did all of that?"

Alanna blinked rapidly and stared at Tia.

"Because he cares about you—that's why," Tia went on. "More than I've ever seen him care about anyone else." Alanna placed one hand on her chest and swallowed hard, and Tia knew she was getting through.

"And do you honestly think he would have done all of that for you just so he could come back here afterward and hang out with Elizabeth? I don't think so."

Alanna's shoulders slumped forward slightly as if she'd just let out a breath she'd been holding in for days. "Oh my God," she said, her voice low. "I can't believe what an idiot I've been."

Join the club, Tia thought.

"You're right," Alanna continued. "All this time Conner's been trying so hard to get through to me, and I've just been . . ."

A wench? Tia thought.

". . . so stubborn."

Close enough. "Yeah, well, it's not too late," Tia told her. "I mean, he sent me over here, so obviously he's still willing to work at it." *As long as he's not the one doing the work,* she thought. What a stupid position she was in. Hadn't she and her friends grown out of the whole find-out-if-he-likes-me thing in sixth grade?

"Do you really think so?" Alanna asked.

"Yeah," Tia said with a shrug. Then, reminding herself once again that this was about Conner and Alanna and that what she thought of their relationship was irrelevant, she added, "Definitely."

"Oh, thank you," Alanna breathed, smiling at Tia for the first time. "Really. Thank you so much for coming over here. I'm going to go over to Conner's and apologize to him as soon as I can. I can't believe how stupid I've been acting. Thanks, Tia."

"Yeah, well. Conner's a good friend. I don't like to see him hurt," Tia said, holding Alanna's gaze.

13

Alanna squinted slightly and opened her mouth to speak, but as far as Tia was concerned, she'd already spent too much of her Saturday morning with Conner's girlfriend.

"So, I'll see you around," Tia said, turning to go.

"Yeah. Thanks again," Alanna said as Tia made her way back down the brick path.

"No problem," Tia called over her shoulder. *At least, not this time,* she thought. But from here on out, Conner and Alanna were on their own. She wasn't about to step in and patch things up for them again.

Why did I agree to meet him here? Melissa thought as she walked into House of Java. Not only was it crowded, but she and Aaron were likely to run into other SVH students. It wasn't exactly the kind of place where she could expect him to make a move.

Then again, meeting where everyone could see them did lend credibility to the idea that she was really just trying to help him with his English grade and nothing more. *You have to find the positives where you can,* Melissa told herself. She was about to step up to the counter and order when she heard someone calling her name.

"Melissa—over here." It was Aaron, and he was

standing about fifteen feet away, near the section of the café where the seating area extended into an L. "I've got a booth in back," he said, gesturing toward the tables around the corner.

In the back, Melissa thought, smiling as she walked toward him. *That sounds cozy.* Maybe Aaron was finally coming around. She walked slowly so that Aaron would have ample opportunity to notice her outfit—low-slung jeans and a close-fitting tee in the style of an old baseball shirt, white with light blue three-quarter sleeves. If there was a more tomboyish outfit around, Melissa hadn't found it yet.

She glanced at the tables to her right and pretended not to notice the way Aaron was eyeing her. She wanted to be absolutely sure he didn't miss one detail, especially the sporty Adidas sneakers that had been sitting at the back of her closet untouched for almost a year now. After all, what was the point of getting all decked out in these ridiculous clothes if Aaron didn't get a good chance to see them?

"I like your shoes," he said as she approached.

Melissa squinted and looked down at them like she wasn't quite sure what he was talking about. Forget the fact that she'd checked herself out in the mirror at least ten times before leaving the house. "Oh. Thanks. I need to get some new ones soon. These are getting pretty worn."

15

"Really? They look almost new," Aaron said.

"Yeah, but the treads are practically gone," Melissa lied. What was he going to do—check her soles?

She followed him around the corner to the very last booth, which, for a crowded Saturday afternoon, actually was rather private. Even better, there were two coffees already on the table.

"I got you one—I hope you don't mind," Aaron said as they sat down. "Cream, no sugar, right?"

Melissa glanced into the mug in front of her. The coffee was a little lighter than she would have made it, but Aaron didn't need to know that. "Perfect," she said, smiling up at him from underneath the brim of her Dodgers cap. Aaron held her gaze for a moment, then cleared his throat and pulled something out of the dark green backpack on his right.

"Good news," he said, handing her a single sheet of paper. "I have an essay test on Monday, and O'Reilly gave us the questions in advance so we could prep for it."

"Great." Melissa nodded, forcing herself to smile as she examined the paper. But it wasn't great at all—at least not for her. For the test, all Aaron had to do was to analyze two poems and explain what literary techniques the poets had used. And according to the sheet of paper in Melissa's hands, students were even allowed to create an outline in advance. How lame was that? Aaron was sure to ace it. How could he not? And with a good grade on this test, he'd be pretty much assured a passing grade for the term, which meant he wouldn't need Melissa to tutor him anymore.

"Isn't this awesome?" Aaron asked. "We're even allowed to bring in an index card with a basic outline on it, as long as it doesn't have any completed sentences or definitions or anything."

"Mm-hmm, I saw that," Melissa said, still focusing on the question. *Who could possibly fail this test?* she wondered. Or even get a grade lower than an A?

"So I figure with you to help me write a killer outline," Aaron went on, "I'll be able to get an A—or at least a high B—and then I should be all set, you know?"

"Yeah, I know," Melissa said, handing him back the paper. "With all the essays we've revised and that extra-credit assignment I helped you with last week—"

"—a good grade on this test would bring my average close to a C. Maybe even a B-minus," Aaron finished, grinning across the table at her. Melissa forced the corners of her mouth upward even as she gritted her teeth.

For practically two weeks now she'd been doing everything she could think of to get Aaron interested enough to make a move—dressing like a tomboy, pretending to like old movies and rap music. She'd even been doing that pathetic snort-laugh thing he found so strangely appealing in a girl. And for a while she'd thought she had him.

He laughed at all of her jokes, even the bad ones, and he was constantly complimenting her—on her clothes, her cheering, her teaching ability, whatever. Plus she was forever catching him staring at her when he didn't think she was paying attention—all moony eyed and drooly. But still, for some reason, he hadn't made a single move. And now Melissa was about to run out of time. *Unless . . .*

"Hey—can I see that again?" Melissa asked, pointing to the paper with the essay question and the index-card guidelines.

"Sure," Aaron said, and when he passed it to her, Melissa noticed that he went out of his way to brush his hand against hers and let it linger there for a minute. He obviously liked her—she just needed a little more time.

"Can I hang on to this so I can jot down some ideas?" she asked.

"Sure."

"Great," Melissa said, folding it in half and tucking it into her bag. "I just want to make sure everything's fresh in my mind before we start prepping."

"Oh, okay." Aaron nodded. "So, then . . . we're not doing it today?"

"No," Melissa said. "I need to think about this some more first. I don't want to let you down."

"I doubt you could," Aaron said, grinning. Melissa stared down at her feet for a minute, pretending his comment had embarrassed her, then smiled back at him.

"How about tomorrow?" Melissa suggested.

"Sounds good. What time?"

"How about eleven—at my house?"

"Perfect," Aaron said, and Melissa had to agree. Twenty-four hours should give her enough time to come up with a way to get Aaron a decent grade on the test so that he would still think she was a good tutor, but one that fell just short of getting him up to the C average he needed to stay on the basketball team. And that would buy her at least another week to work with him on the stuff that really mattered. Like kissing her. And showing Will and Cherie exactly how it felt to be betrayed.

"I just don't think it's smart, that's all," Tia said, flopping down on the bright orange couch in Andy's basement.

"Why?" Andy asked. He took a handful of popcorn from the bowl his mom had brought down and threw a piece into the air, catching it in his mouth.

"Nice," Tia said with a nod.

"What can I say?" Andy replied. "I'm gifted. So why don't you think Conner and Alanna should be together?" he asked. Tia had been brooding about her role in reuniting them ever since she'd arrived nearly an hour ago, but so far, Andy hadn't heard her give one concrete reason why she was so against it.

"I don't know," Tia said. "I just—" She sighed and ran one hand through her long, brown hair, then wrinkled her nose. "Do you know what I think it is?" she asked finally.

"No," Andy replied, "but I'm dying to hear what you've come up with this time." Tia took a piece of popcorn and threw it at him, scowling. "I just don't think Conner should be dating someone so unstable."

"Yeah," Andy said, nodding. "You're right, you know? Because Conner is such a model of stability himself. I'd hate to see someone throw off his perfect balance."

Tia clicked her tongue. "You're such a jerk," she said. "That's not what I meant. I was just saying—"

"Sorry," Andy interrupted, pointing toward the cordless phone, which had just started ringing. "I have to take this." He walked over to the pool table and grabbed the receiver. "Hello?"

"Hey, Andy, it's Dave—guess what?"

"Um . . . Tom Cruise finally came out of the closet?"

"No," Dave said with a laugh. "It's better than that."

"Better than Tom Cruise?" Andy said. "Oh, I know— *Brad Pitt* just came out of the closet."

"No," Dave said. "Nobody came out of the closet."

"That's too bad. So what's up?" Andy asked.

"Well, I just got a letter from the American Association for Aspiring Attorneys," Dave said, "and I won that scholarship I applied for last semester!"

Andy felt something tighten in the pit of his stomach. "Wow, that's . . . great," he said. "Congratulations."

"Thanks. I'm pretty psyched."

"What is it?" Tia asked, sitting bolt upright on the couch. "What happened?"

Dave chuckled. "Hey, tell Tia I said hi."

"Gee, how'd you know she was here?" Andy droned, glancing sideways at Tia, who was now standing right next to him.

"Congratulations on what?" she asked, tugging at Andy's arm.

Andy tilted the mouthpiece of the phone away from his face. "Dave won a scholarship," he explained.

"Awesome—congratulations, Dave!" Tia said, leaning over to yell into the phone.

"Tell her I said thanks," Dave replied.

"He says thanks," Andy said, glaring at Tia. He hated talking on the phone when she was around.

She needed the full play-by-play. And he hated it even more when the conversation was about *another* one of his friends receiving some kind of award or honor. Not that they didn't deserve all these awards and honors. It was just that everyone seemed to be winning something. Everyone except Andy.

"We should celebrate," Tia suggested. "Me and Trent and the two of you—we could go out for dinner or something."

Andy winced and covered the phone with his hand, but it was too late.

"That's a good idea," Dave said. "Isn't it, Andy?"

"Sure. Great," Andy replied, but as he spoke, he narrowed his eyes at Tia.

"What?" she whispered, squinting back at him, but Andy waved her off.

"What time?" Dave asked.

"I don't know," Andy said. "What time, Tia?"

"Six?" Tia said with a shrug. Then she mouthed, *What's wrong?* at Andy.

Andy shook his head. "How about six?" he asked.

"Sounds good. I'll meet you at your house and we can go from there," Dave said.

"Okay," Andy agreed. "Oh—and congratulations again. That's really great."

"Thanks. I'll talk to you later," Dave said.

"Okay, see ya," Andy replied, and as soon as he had hung up the phone, Tia was on him.

"What's going on?" she asked. "Why are you so grumpy all of a sudden?"

"I'm not grumpy," Andy said, rolling his eyes.

"Well, something's bugging you," Tia responded. "What is it? Don't you want to go out to dinner? Or did you just want to hang out with Dave—without me and Trent, I mean? Because if that's what it is, that's fine. We don't have to go."

"No, that's not it," Andy said. He walked back over to the couch and sat down, sinking into the overstuffed cushions.

"What, then?" Tia asked, following him. She perched herself on the armrest facing him and stared, waiting.

"It's stupid," Andy said, trying to ignore the voice inside his head that kept telling him what a loser he was.

"Try me."

Andy glanced up at Tia, whose eyes were still on him, her gaze unwavering. "All right," he said with a heavy sigh. "It's just . . . I don't know. It's stupid. I'm just sick of being the underachiever around here."

"*Underachiever?*" Tia repeated. "Where do you get *that*?"

"Oh, gee, I don't know," Andy said. "Maybe from

23

the fact that I'm the only one not being offered full tuition to the college of my choice or special auditions for exclusive performing-arts schools."

Tia squinted. "I haven't been offered anything like that either," she said.

"Yes, you have. What about the Senate scholarship?"

"Maria won that, not me."

"Yeah, but you were nominated," Andy protested. "Which means you're one of the top students at SVH, and you're probably going to be offered plenty of other scholarships before the year's over."

"I don't know about that." Tia cocked her head.

"Still," Andy said, "at least you've been nominated for something. And didn't Trent get some kind of award at his sports banquet last week?"

"Yeah, but—"

"And Conner had that audition, and now Dave's got this lawyer-scholarship thing." Andy shook his head. "I told you—it's stupid."

"It's not stupid, Andy," Tia assured him.

"Yeah. It is," Andy insisted. "So you know what? Forget I said anything about it." Andy stared down at his hands and started fidgeting to get a piece of dirt out from under one of his fingernails. He knew Tia was still staring at him, but he didn't want to look up. He felt like such a baby, whining about himself when Dave had just been given this great award.

"What if I call Dave and tell him tonight's not good for me and Trent?" Tia suggested. "Maybe he'd be up for doing it some other night."

"Nah," Andy said. "Really. Just forget what I said. I'll get over it, and you're right—this is a big deal for Dave. We should definitely go out and celebrate."

"Are you sure?" Tia asked. She leaned sideways to get a better look at Andy's face.

"Yeah," Andy said. He finished cleaning under his fingernail, then clapped and stood up. "I think I'm going to grab a shower before we go," he said.

"Yeah. I should go home and call Trent and change," Tia agreed. "So we're meeting back here at six, right?"

"Right," Andy said, forcing half a smile onto his face. "And don't worry—I'll be ready to celebrate by then."

Tia bit her lip and scrutinized his face. "Are you sure?" she asked. "Because I can call it off without making anyone suspicious. I'm good at being sneaky."

Andy shook his head and waved her off. "I'll be fine," he said. "Going out will cheer me up." Tia pressed her lips together, still staring at him. "And besides," Andy added, "I really am happy for Dave. This scholarship's a big deal, you know."

Tia nodded slowly and smiled. "Good attitude,

Andy," she said. "I'm proud of you." She gave him a peck on the cheek, then turned and headed upstairs. "I'll see you at six," she called.

"Yeah. Six," Andy said. "Perfect."

He flopped back onto the sofa and tried to console himself. At least he had plans for the night. That was something, wasn't it? And with the way his friends kept racking up the awards, his social calendar was likely to be full with celebration parties through the end of the year. Which was a good thing, because it didn't look like anything worth celebrating was going to happen to him anytime soon.

Melissa Fox

This is going to be such an easy essay. O'Reilly even gave them the poems in advance— what kind of test is that? It sounds like the kind of thing we would have done back in sophomore English at El Carro with Mr. Cheever. He was always giving us study guides for tests and quizzes and stuff because, as he told us over and over again, all he cared about was whether we grasped the information. Actually, now that I think about it, I did learn a lot in his class. But that's not the point.

The point is I need Aaron to get a B-minus or worse. But with the essay questions and the poems

in advance and me to help him
study, he'd have to completely
choke for that to happen. He'd
have to either mess up all the
terms or totally leave them out,
which is . . . wait a second.

Wasn't it O'Reilly that Will
was complaining about the other
day? Yeah, I'm sure it was. He
was saying she didn't seem to
care what he wrote or how he
wrote it as long as he got all
the right buzzwords into his
essays. I remember because he
showed me one of his papers—
something he'd written on _The
Sun Also Rises_—and she had
actually made little red check
marks whenever he used a term
she'd mentioned in class. _Lost
Generation_—check. _Realism_—
check. _Suicide_—check. Will called
it the "glance-and-grade" system,

and he got all indignant about it since he's such a serious writer now. Ha.

But if that's really how she grades, I just might be able to pull this off. I can help Aaron put together all the right information, which will make me look good, but I'll keep the focus on the explanations—not the terms. Then his essay will be technically correct, but when O'Reilly skims it for buzzwords like _assonance_ and _onomatopoeia_ she won't find any. She'll give him a low grade, he'll blame it on her and not me, and I'll get to keep tutoring him. It's perfect.

Or at least it will be—when Aaron hooks up with me, and Will and Cherie get left out in the cold.

CHAPTER

Addicted to Love

2

A meeting, Alanna thought, applying a little more pressure to the gas pedal. Conner never attended meetings on weekends—unless, of course, he was feeling really shaky.

Which if he is, it's totally my fault.

She glanced at the clock on her dashboard. Five forty-three, and she was stuck behind what had to be the slowest car in town. "Pick a lane," Alanna snarled, gripping the steering wheel as—one millimeter at a time—the white Mercedes in front of her edged to the right.

"Not that one!" Alanna groaned, following it into the turning lane. She could see the sign for the El Carro Community Resource Center in the distance, but at this speed she wouldn't reach it until next Tuesday.

She drummed her fingers on the steering wheel—hands at ten and two, just like Mr. King had taught her in driver's ed, and forced herself to ease off the accelerator. What was it Mr. King always used to say? *You're not going to get there any faster by driving three inches away from his bumper*. Yeah, that was it. But with only twelve minutes to go till meeting-time, Alanna couldn't help thinking that every inch of road counted.

Finally they reached the entrance for the community center. But just as Alanna was beginning to think she was going to make it, the Mercedes stopped and put on its turn signal. Its *left* turn signal.

"Oh, come on," Alanna wailed. "You've got to be kidding!" She dropped her head back against the top of her seat and moaned as cars whizzed by in the left lane. If there really were such a thing as a citizen's arrest, she was ready to make one. For what, she wasn't sure. *Bad driving? Slow driving? Just plain stupid driving?* There had to be some rule this idiot was breaking by causing what should have been a five-minute drive to take her twenty.

"Just go, already," she said, watching as the Mercedes missed opportunity after opportunity to pull into traffic. Five forty-eight. She didn't have time for this.

"So long, Grandma," Alanna muttered, cutting her wheel sharply to the right and barreling around the Mercedes on the half-paved, half-gravel shoulder. She glanced left as she went by, expecting to see

31

a blue-haired old lady hunched over the wheel, but to her surprise, the driver was a girl about her age.

Huh. Probably nervous about scratching up Daddy's car, Alanna thought. She pulled into the community center, scanning the lot for Conner's car. Five forty-nine. *He's probably already inside,* she told herself, but then she spotted him. He was sitting on the hood of his black Mustang, leaning back against the windshield with his eyes closed. *Oh, thank God I made it,* Alanna thought, her heart pounding. *But what is he doing?*

As she drove nearer, she realized his radio was on—loud. She pulled into the space next to his, half excited to see him, half worried that he'd stalk off as soon as he noticed her. Or roll his eyes. Or do something to show he was less than happy to see her. But he didn't even flinch. He just lay there, his eyes still closed, and for a moment she thought he might be asleep.

Alanna hopped out of her car and ran around the front, her clogs clunking against the pavement, but it wasn't until she was practically next to him that he finally squinted his eyes open and placed one hand on his forehead to shield them from the sun.

"Alanna?"

"I know—I'm probably the last person you want to see right now, but—"

"How did you—?"

"Megan," Alanna answered. "I stopped by your house and she told me where you were."

Conner sat up and swung his legs over the side of the car, letting them dangle there. Alanna stepped forward so that they were more or less face-to-face, but she was careful not to get too close until she'd had a chance to explain herself.

"So what's up?" he asked.

"I wanted to apologize. I've been a complete jerk, and I'm so sorry. I never should have gotten so upset about Chicago, not to mention Elizabeth. I know you're just friends, and I know you really were working on some kind of writing thing, and I never should have doubted you. I just . . ."

Conner narrowed his eyes. "What?"

"I don't know. It's like . . . I'm not used to having things work out, you know? Having people stick around. I keep waiting for you to wake up and realize . . . I don't know . . . what a big mistake you're making, I guess." Alanna stared down at her shoes, fixating on the scuff marks at the outer edges of her soles. She had a habit of rolling her ankles out when she was standing, which always caused her shoes to wear in strange places. "I'm not making sense, am I?" she asked, venturing an upward glance. But instead of the cold stare she had expected, Conner was actually smirking.

"Come here," he said, one arm outstretched. Alanna placed her hand in his, and he pulled her close, enveloping her in a hug that made her wish she could stop time. She rested her chin against his shoulder and pressed her eyes closed, hoping this wasn't just a dream. Or if it was, that she never had to wake up.

"You mean you don't hate me?" she asked after a moment, her voice muffled by his dark blue sweatshirt.

"Nah."

"Not even a little?"

Conner shook his head. Then he smoothed her curly auburn hair with one hand, his breath tickling her forehead.

"Because I really am sorry. I never should have given you such a hard time about bringing my parents to Chicago—I know you were just trying to help. And the whole Elizabeth thing . . . I was wrong about that too. I just—"

"Shhh," Conner whispered. He tightened his arms around her, and Alanna let herself sink into him even deeper. He felt so good. So safe.

"Tia came to talk to me this morning," she said.

"I know."

Alanna pulled back and smiled up at him. "You know everything, don't you?"

"Pretty much." Conner nodded, and the two of them laughed. Alanna gazed into his green eyes for a

34

moment, feeling like she was seeing them for the first time. They were such a beautiful shade of green, with brownish gold flecks at the center. Intense and soulful—hardened and vulnerable all at once. She stood on her toes and leaned closer, and when her lips met his, she wasn't quite certain who had kissed who. Not that it mattered.

"Five fifty-five," a nearby voice called, causing Alanna to jump. She and Conner both turned toward the sound of shuffling feet and saw a stout man in his forties or fifties walking by. He wore a navy blue wool captain's hat despite the balmy weather, and Alanna recognized him from past meetings.

"Thanks," Conner called, and the guy waved back at them. "I better go," he said.

Alanna blinked rapidly. "Still?" she asked. She'd assumed that since things were patched up between the two of them, Conner wouldn't need to go to the meeting.

"Yeah. You want to come?"

"I don't know," Alanna said, narrowing her eyes.

"Come on," Conner said, hopping off his car. "It'll be fun," he added in a mocking tone.

"Oh, right. I forgot," Alanna responded sarcastically. A.A. meetings weren't exactly her favorite hangout, but being with Conner—anywhere—was.

By the time they got inside, the meeting was just about to start. There were about thirteen people already seated in the ring of chairs at the center of the room and a few more milling about. Conner led Alanna over to two chairs on the far side of the circle, and they sat down just as the facilitator was calling everybody to order.

"Just a few quick announcements and then we'll let our speaker, Lesley, begin."

Alanna leaned closer to Conner. "This is an open meeting, right?"

"Yeah."

Good, Alanna thought. That meant anyone could attend and not everyone there was necessarily an alcoholic—which meant nobody knew for certain that *she* was an alcoholic, and that's the way she liked it. She hadn't been able to make herself attend a closed meeting yet, though she was pretty sure Conner had been to a few. Maybe now that they were back together, she could work up the nerve to go to one—as long as he went with her.

". . . and we'll be adding a Tuesday night meeting to our regular schedule starting next week," the facilitator was saying, but Alanna was only half listening. Instead she was staring at Conner's jawline. It was so sharp and angular, and she loved the distinct line it cut between his cheek and the upper part of his throat. Not to mention how sexy it looked when he'd gone a few days without shaving.

"Hi. I'm Lesley Fine," a new voice said, and Alanna realized the speaker had begun. Even so, she had a hard time looking away from Conner. Why had they come to this meeting anyway? It wasn't like either one of them had been drinking lately. She would have much preferred to just go for coffee or something—somewhere where they could sit in a booth or on a comfy couch, and she could reach over and touch his hand or cuddle into his arms. Anywhere but here.

". . . but after a year of slips—and I mean more than just a few—I realized it just wasn't healthy for me. He was a great guy, but I wasn't ready. I plunged into that relationship after only a week of sobriety, and as a result I never learned to stand on my own. It was like I replaced my addiction to alcohol with an addiction to another person."

For the first time Alanna turned to face the speaker. She was an attractive woman with curly black hair and dark brown eyes. *Early forties, probably,* Alanna guessed, though she'd noticed that a lot of the people she'd met at A.A. meetings looked older than they actually were. *Maybe midthirties.*

"That's probably why my sponsor encouraged me early on to take it slow. I remember her saying it was a good idea to resist starting new relationships or making too many life changes during the first year of sobriety, but it was like I just couldn't help it.

Falling in love felt so good. It was hard for me to believe anything bad could ever come of it. But what I failed to realize was that I wasn't falling in love—I was just filling a void."

Lesley went on to discuss the specifics of her recovery and how she was dealing with things now—five years later—but Alanna couldn't get her mind off what she'd just heard. *No new relationships during the first year of sobriety? Is that, like, an A.A. rule or something?* she wondered. Because if it was, she was obviously violating it—and so was Conner.

She glanced over at him, wishing she could grab his hand and give it a squeeze so she could tell if he was as freaked out by this news as she was, but she didn't want to draw attention to their relationship. Especially if someone might advise her to put it on hold for a year. If she had to do that, there was no way she could stay sober. She'd rather quit A.A. than give up Conner.

She just hoped he felt the same way.

"Wait—what was that?" Trent said, pointing at the television screen.

Tia clicked back two channels and paused. "This? The Ronco food dehydrator?"

"Ooh—make your own beef jerky!" Andy said, rubbing his hands together. "Quick, Dave, write down the phone number." Dave grabbed a notepad from the overturned wooden crate that served as a coffee table in Andy's basement and pretended to scribble something down.

"*Nooo,* not the infomercial. One more," Trent told Tia.

Tia pressed the remote again and landed on ESPN2, which was broadcasting some kind of golf tournament. "No way," she said, immediately skipping up through the channels again.

"Oh, come on," Trent pleaded. "Tiger's playing."

"Uh-uh," Tia said. "Golf is way too boring for a Saturday night."

"Golf isn't boring," Trent protested.

"Oh, not at all," Andy agreed. "Wait. I think they're about to announce which club the golfer is going to use." He held up his fist, as if he were grasping a microphone, and spoke in a hushed tone. "It looks like he's going for the number-nine chipper—an excellent choice for this particular bunker. It should allow him to arc the ball out of the sand and onto the green without overshooting, but only if he hits it perfectly. This is an important shot. All right. Now he's lining up his shot, examining it from all angles, and . . . it looks like he's going to have a chat with his caddy. Well, while they confer, I'll just read to you from the *Encyclopaedia Britannica* to keep you entertained."

Trent shook his head. "Come on. It's not that bad," he said, grinning slightly in spite of Andy's mockery.

"You're right," Andy said. "I'm exaggerating. Plus there's that part between holes where you get to watch them all walk to the next one—now, *that's* excitement."

"Okay, fine." Trent chuckled. "No golf."

"I don't believe it!" Tia exclaimed suddenly, causing all of them to turn toward the television. "Andy— isn't that the guy we saw in New York?"

Andy squinted at the TV, then dropped his jaw. "Oh, wow," he said. "Yeah—Frank Falcon." Tia had stopped on a comedy channel that was showing stand-up live from the Improv. "I can't believe he's actually on here."

The four of them listened for a minute while Frank made a few recycled jokes about the New York Stock Exchange. Somehow these little blasts from the past managed to elicit a laugh or two from the audience.

Tia tilted her head. "He's a little better," she said.

"But not much," Andy replied.

"You guys saw him in New York?" Dave asked.

"Yeah, when we did that game show at QTV," Tia said. "He was at an open-mike night we went to, and he practically got booed offstage. Andy was ten thousand times funnier when he went up."

"You went up *onstage?*" Dave said, turning to Andy.

Andy shrugged one shoulder. "Yeah."

"And he was incredible!" Tia gushed. "The audience loved him, and if we'd been in town longer, I swear the club manager would have offered him a regular spot or something."

"That's awesome, Andy," Trent said. "How come you never told us?"

"Yeah," Dave interjected. "How come you never told me about that?"

"I don't know," Andy said. He shot a quick glare at Tia, but she just grinned.

"He gets all shy about it for some reason," Tia said. "He wasn't even going to go up until the manager and I made him."

"You didn't *make* me," Andy said.

"Okay. So we didn't have to physically drag him up there, but still, he didn't exactly volunteer on his own."

Andy rolled his eyes. Why did Tia have to make everything sound so dramatic? So he'd done stand-up. Once. And he hadn't been pelted with tomatoes. It wasn't like he'd found a cure for cancer or anything.

"Wow. You should go to the open-mike night at that club in Big Mesa, the Sierra," Dave said. "I'd love to see your routine."

"Me too," agreed Trent.

"I don't *have* a routine," Andy said.

"You could write one," Dave suggested.

"Yeah." Trent nodded. "You could even use all that stuff you just said about golf."

Andy winced. "It wouldn't be funny out of context."

"Sure, it would," Tia said, "if *you* said it. You're hilarious, Andy. Don't you get that?"

"She's right," Dave agreed. "You're one of the funniest people I know. Your stories always make me laugh, but when I try to tell them to other people, they never come out right. There's something about your delivery or your timing or something. I don't know."

"You should go for it, man," Trent said. "If you made a roomful of people laugh after they sat through this Falcon guy, you must be good."

"He is," Tia insisted.

Andy shook his head. "I don't know," he said. "I mean, it was kind of a onetime thing, you know?"

"But you loved it," Tia protested. "You were on such a high coming out of that club—you really ought to give it another shot."

"Yeah, maybe," Andy said. He knew Tia was right—about the way he'd felt in New York, at least. Walking off that stage, he'd felt ready to take on the world. He remembered thinking that must be the way an athlete who scored the winning point for his team in the final seconds of a game felt—like he was some kind of hero who could do anything. But that was then, and it had also been under special circumstances. They were in New York, where no one knew him and he had nothing to lose. And he'd only done it once. Who was to say he could ever be funny in front of a crowd again?

"They do the open-mike thing every Sunday and Wednesday," Dave said. "And anyone can go up there. You should give it a try."

Andy shrugged. "Maybe I will," he said, focusing on the TV just as Frank Falcon was leaving and another comedian was being introduced. "Hey—I've seen this guy on another channel before," Andy said, pointing at the screen. "He's really good. Turn it up."

Tia increased the volume, and to Andy's relief, his friends all seemed to be paying attention to the television now instead of planning out his stand-up career. Hopefully they'd forget about it altogether—at least for the rest of the night.

But as Andy watched the comedian who was onstage now, he couldn't help remembering how it felt to be up there under the lights—not to mention what a rush it was when the audience actually laughed at his jokes.

Maybe stand-up was something he should try

out again, just to see. Because if that night in New York hadn't been a complete fluke, his friends could be right. He might have a talent for comedy. And that would be worth celebrating.

"I'm so glad I caught up with you tonight," Alanna said as she and Conner strolled through a semiwooded section of the park.

"Yeah. Me too," Conner agreed. He walked over to a bench with dark green paint that shone in the late day sun and took a seat. Alanna sat next to him and scooted over until her leg was pressed against his and she could rest her head on his shoulder.

Conner put his arm around her and nuzzled the top of her head with his chin. "New shampoo?" he asked.

"Yeah. My mom went a little overboard at The Body Shop. What do you think?"

Conner buried his nose in Alanna's curly hair and sniffed. "Nice," he said, kissing her head softly.

"It's lavender scented," Alanna replied. "And so are the conditioner, the body wash, the after-bath spray, the lotion, the aromatherapy candle—"

"She bought you all that stuff?"

"Mm-hmm. Yesterday. She thought I seemed a little stressed out, and I guess lavender is supposed to help you relax—at least that's what it says on all the containers."

"Did it work?" Conner asked.

"A little," Alanna said with a shrug. "But this is working a whole lot more," she added, snuggling into him. Conner gave her a gentle squeeze and leaned down to kiss her just as Alanna was tilting her head up to do the same thing. Their eyes met for a moment, and they both smiled; then Alanna felt Conner's soft lips pressing into hers, and she closed her eyes.

Kissing Conner was different from kissing any other guy she'd ever known. Not that she'd kissed a ton of guys, but she'd kissed enough to know that Conner was something special.

Alanna shivered as the tingling sensation that had started in her lips spread throughout the rest of her body. Conner's kisses always affected her that way, making her feel excited all over—but there was also a certain amount of comfort involved. Kissing Conner felt warm and safe. It felt right.

She sighed as Conner pulled away, angling himself so that they were sitting almost face-to-face now. He was just about to lean in and kiss her again when the image of Lesley, who had spoken at their A.A. meeting, flashed through Alanna's mind.

"Hey—what did you think of that speaker tonight?" she asked suddenly.

Conner stopped short. "Huh?"

"I'm sorry." Alanna shook her head. "I don't mean to kill the mood or anything, but I can't get all of that stuff she said out of my mind."

"What stuff?" Conner asked, drawing back.

"You know," Alanna started. She was a little hesitant to bring it up—she didn't want to give Conner any reason to think their relationship was a bad thing if he wasn't already thinking it—but at the same time she couldn't just let it go.

"What? About how she got sober?" Conner guessed.

"Yeah, *that*, but . . . I don't know," Alanna hedged. "I just keep thinking about how she said she almost *didn't* get sober. You know, like how she said that when she was dating that guy, she used to start drinking again every time things weren't going well?" Conner nodded. "And she seemed to think it was because she started dating him before she was ready. How did she put it?" Alanna bit her lip and squinted. "Oh—I remember. She said it was like she had replaced one addiction with another." She watched Conner's face closely, but he didn't even blink.

"So?" he asked.

Alanna sighed. "*So-ooo*, she said she should have waited longer—like a year or something—before she started dating."

"Uh-huh," Conner said, nodding again.

Alanna stared at him. "*Well . . . ?* What did you think of that?"

Conner shrugged. "I think she's right."

"You do?"

"Sure," Conner said with a shrug. "She should have waited a little longer."

Alanna's mouth dropped open. "How can you say that so easily? Like it's no big deal?"

Conner drew back and glanced sideways at her. "*Is* it a big deal?" he asked.

"Of course it is," Alanna said.

Conner narrowed his eyes. "Why?" he asked.

"Because *we're* just getting sober," Alanna explained.

"So?"

"Isn't it obvious?" Alanna asked. "We met at *rehab,* of all places, and everyone in A.A.—including you—seems to think that people should avoid dating during their first year."

"I didn't say that."

"Yes, you did," Alanna insisted. "You said that Lesley was right and that she would have been better off if she had waited to date."

"Right. I said *Lesley* would have been better off. I wasn't talking about us."

"But how are we any different?" Alanna demanded. "I've already done some of the stuff she was talking about. Like when we'd just gotten back from rehab and I thought you were blowing me off, remember? I started drinking again."

"And then you stopped," Conner said. "Besides, that wasn't all because of us. You were having a hard time with your parents because they were still acting like nothing had happened. Remember?"

Alanna rolled her eyes. "How could I forget? They paraded me around the country club like I'd just gotten back from charm school or something, and then we had to meet up with my uncle and a bunch of the neighbors for dessert."

"Cupcakes," Conner said with a nod.

"Yeah, cupcakes," Alanna said, grinning slightly.

Conner reached over and brushed a strand of hair off her face, tucking it behind her ear, and Alanna leaned her cheek against his hand.

"How do your hands always stay so warm?" she asked.

"Good circulation," he said, bending and unbending his fingers a few times. "From playing guitar."

"Ah." Alanna nodded. They sat silently for a few minutes, watching the sun as it sank farther and farther below the horizon.

"So," Alanna said finally. "You really think that we're okay?"

"Uh-huh," Conner answered.

"And it doesn't bother you that everyone else at

48

that meeting seemed to think that dating right away is a bad idea?"

"No," Conner said.

Alanna smiled. "You don't know how happy I am to hear you say that," she said, wrapping her arms around him. She felt his breath on her neck and his arms around her and couldn't help wondering how she'd gotten so lucky. Conner was amazing, and for some strange reason, he still wanted to be with her. Even after she'd acted like a complete idiot about Chicago and Elizabeth *and* despite everything Lesley had said about dating in the first year of sobriety.

She squeezed him tighter, thankful for his strength and confidence. And his ability to do what he thought was right even when other people disagreed.

Now, if I can just stop worrying about what everybody else thinks, Alanna told herself, *we just might make it.*

Conner McDermott

The A.A. Twelve-Step pamphlet doesn't say anything about dating. Or not dating. I checked. Alanna's just taking all that stuff the speaker said way too personally.

But even if there was some kind of rule, who's to say that we'd have to follow it? A.A. is about finding your own way to make things work. It's not about telling you exactly what to do and when to do it.

Sure, it's a twelve-step program, but that doesn't mean everyone has to do all twelve steps exactly the same way. Some people might even need thirteen. If Alanna and I can stay sober, that's all that matters.

At least, that's the way I see it.

CHAPTER 3
Buying Time

Othello: Now, by heaven, My blood begins my
safer guides to rule, And passion,
having my best judgment collied,
Assays to lead the way.

Huh?

Alanna read the passage over three times, but it
didn't get any clearer. *Why couldn't Shakespeare
have just said what he meant? Because if he had,*
Alanna thought, *high-school English teachers would
have to find a different way to torture their students.*

Of course, the worst part of reading *Othello* was
that she was doing it alone. The rest of her class had
read it while she was in rehab, and now she was
stuck playing catch-up, which meant she had to get
through the whole play and complete all the assignments without the benefit of class discussion.

Sure, her English teacher, Ms. Hamlin, had given
her copies of class notes and offered to meet with

51

her whenever she wanted, but that didn't make things any easier. She'd managed to get back on track in most of her other classes by now, but she still had work to make up for Spanish and chemistry too. She didn't exactly have a lot of free time.

Just as she was about to read through Othello's passage a fourth time, there was a knock at the door. "Come in," Alanna called. When the door swung open, she saw her father standing there, and he didn't look happy. His face was red, as though he had sprinted up and down the front staircase twelve times before coming to her room.

"Alanna—what do you call this?" he demanded, waving an envelope in the air.

"Um . . . a letter?" Alanna guessed.

"An *unfinished* letter," Mr. Feldman corrected her. Alanna raised one eyebrow, wondering for a moment if her father had finally gone off the deep end, but then it hit her exactly which letter he was talking about. It was supposed to be an apology to the Bresinskys, whose house she'd stayed at when she'd run away, but so far all she'd managed to do was address the envelope.

"Where did you find that?" she asked.

"On the kitchen table—right where you left it," her father said. His deep voice resonated in Alanna's ears.

"Oh," Alanna said, wondering how she could have been so stupid.

"You told me you'd finished this letter and mailed it. *A week ago.*"

Alanna pressed her eyes shut and took a deep breath. *Stupid, stupid, stupid!* she admonished herself. How could she have just left it sitting there? "I know. I'm sorry," she said quietly. "I just didn't want you to—"

"Know the truth?" Mr. Feldman cut in.

"*Nooo.* Get upset," Alanna told him.

"So you lied to me."

"I didn't lie. I meant to finish the letter; I just—"

"You just *what?*" Mr. Feldman snapped. "Had to make a phone call? Or watch your favorite TV show?"

"No!" Alanna yelled, glaring up at her father. "Is that what you think I've been doing?"

"I don't know what you've been doing. I only know what you *haven't* been doing," Mr. Feldman said, "and the list is getting rather long."

Alanna's jaw dropped. "What's that supposed to mean?"

"It means that I asked you to do one simple thing—apologize to the Bresinskys—and not only did you *not* do it, you lied to me about it."

"And I'm *sorry,*" Alanna insisted. "But still, that's just one thing. What do you mean, 'the list is getting long'?"

"Do you want examples?" her father asked, but he didn't wait for her to answer. "You treat our home like a boardinghouse, coming and going as you please; you never leave notes, despite the fact that your mother has asked you to. And then, when you *are* home," he continued, ticking the items off on his fingers, "you hide yourself away up here in your room, which, incidentally, is a mess. Mrs. Murphy can't even vacuum in here, let alone determine which piles of clothing are clean and which are dirty. But has anyone asked you to clean it up? No. And do you know why?"

Alanna clenched her teeth and forced herself to hold her father's gaze.

"Because no one dares," he said. "You walk around this house with a permanent frown, brooding about who knows what, and you can't even put a pleasant expression on your face when your mother and I take you to the club for dinner."

"Maybe that's because I don't *like* going to the club for dinner," Alanna snapped.

"You don't seem to *like* much of anything these days," Mr. Feldman replied. "Except feeling sorry for yourself—that's a sentiment you've embraced wholeheartedly."

Alanna gaped at her father, the tightness in her chest making her feel like she was about to erupt. "I am *not* feeling sorry for myself!" she yelled. "What do you expect from me anyway? I'm doing everything I can to catch up in school and stay on the right track, but—"

"I don't want to hear it," her father said. "I'm tired of all the excuses, Alanna."

"I'm not making excuses! Don't you understand how hard it is for me to—"

"That's enough, Alanna. I said I don't want to hear it."

"But—"

"But nothing. One of these days you're going to have to stop playing the victim and start taking responsibility for your actions," Mr. Feldman said. He tossed the envelope addressed to the Bresinskys and its blank note card onto Alanna's bed. "I want that letter finished. Today."

"But I—"

"No excuses. Just do it," Mr. Feldman said, and before Alanna could protest, he walked out, pulling the door closed behind him.

Alanna picked up the letter and hurled it after him, but it only went halfway to the door before it got caught in the air and twirled its way down to the rose-colored carpet. "Jerk," she muttered, her cheeks flaring. She grabbed the pillow from her bed and threw it at the door, then walked over to a pile of neatly folded laundry and kicked it until the clothes were scattered around her room. "There," she said. "*Now* it's messy."

She walked back to her bed and sat down heavily, replaying her father's words over and over in her head. How could he be so cold? So cruel? *So wrong?* He obviously thought she was just lazy. But how could he believe that? Didn't he realize how difficult things had been for her ever since she'd gotten back from rehab? How hard it was to catch up on all her homework and attend A.A. meetings at the same time? How hard it was to write an apology to the Bresinskys when she felt so stupid about the whole thing that she didn't even know where to start? How hard it was just to get up each morning, trying to stay sober while everyone placed more and more demands on her?

And she didn't have anyone she could talk to about it. It was like she was in her own little stress bubble, and no one else had a clue what she was going through. *Well . . . almost no one,* Alanna thought. She picked up the phone and dialed Conner's number.

"Hello?"

"Conner?"

"Yeah."

"It's Alanna. I—" Her voice wavered, and suddenly Alanna realized she was on the verge of tears.

"Alanna? Are you okay? What's going on?" Conner asked.

Alanna inhaled deeply, her breath shuddering in her chest. "I'm fine," she said. "Just a little shaken up."

"What happened?"

"Nothing. I just had a big fight with my dad, that's all."

"Oh," Conner said. "What about?"

"The usual. You know, how irresponsible I am and what a disappointment I am to this family," Alanna said.

"That stuff again, huh?"

"Yeah. It's his favorite theme."

"Well, at least you know not to take him seriously," Conner said.

"What do you mean?"

"Just that you can't believe the stuff your father says when he's angry—he's just blowing off steam."

"Maybe," Alanna said with a sigh, "but that doesn't make it any easier to hear. It still hurts, you know."

"Don't let it get to you," Conner said, like it was no big deal.

"How can I not?" Alanna asked. "I have to live in the same house with him, knowing that he thinks I'm lazy and that all I ever do is sit around feeling sorry for myself."

"But that's not true," Conner said.

"*He* thinks it is."

"So?"

Alanna scrunched up her face. "What do you mean, 'so'?"

"I mean, why does it matter so much what someone else thinks of you?"

"Uh, gee—maybe because he's my *father?*" she suggested.

"Still, you can't take everything he says so personally."

"Oh, really? And just how am I supposed to take it?" Alanna snapped.

"I don't know," Conner said. "But you can't keep overreacting every time he says something like this to you. You're going to drive yourself crazy."

"Overreacting?" Alanna repeated. "You think I'm overreacting?"

"Look, Alanna, I just think you need to—"

"You know what?" Alanna interrupted. "Forget it. You're right. I'll be fine. I just need to get over it and let it go. Thanks. I'll talk to you later," she added, and before Conner could respond, she pressed the off button on her cordless phone and threw the receiver down on her bed.

The problem was she wasn't going to just get over it. She was still reeling from all the things her father had said to her, and now she was fuming about Conner's insensitivity too. Alanna picked up the phone again. If only she could find someone who would just listen and sympathize without telling her what she was doing wrong. But who? She stared at the numbers on the phone face and tried to think of someone she could call.

Marissa? No. She was a school friend—one Alanna could call for rides or homework assignments, but not much else. In fact, that's the way most of Alanna's friendships were. She hadn't shared the details of her personal life with any of them. They were all more like acquaintances than friends—except for Lisa. But she'd already leaned on Lisa, and Lisa's parents, enough.

Who, then? Alanna wondered. There really wasn't anyone else. The people she'd met at her local A.A. meetings were pretty good listeners, but she didn't even know any of their last names, let alone their phone numbers. Or did she?

She ran over to her backpack and began rifling through it. If she remembered right, she'd been given the name of a woman who was supposed to be her interim sponsor until she developed a relationship with someone in A.A. who could fill the role permanently.

She emptied out her bag—books, notepads, pens, pencils, a graphing calculator, an unfinished box of animal crackers, and finally, way at the bottom, crumpled up and covered in crumbs, a slip of paper with a name and a number.

Sandra Bietche. I wonder if that's pronounced the way it looks, Alanna thought as she punched in the numbers on her phone.

"Hi, this is Sandra. You know the drill," said a cheerful voice, and it was followed immediately by a beep. Alanna opened her mouth to speak, but no sound came out. What was she supposed to say? "Hello, my name is Alanna, and I'm an alcoholic"? No way.

Instead she hung up. She'd have to be totally desperate before she started whining about her problems to some unknown person's answering machine. Especially when the answering machine belonged to someone named Sandy Bietche. That was almost as bad as a girl Alanna had known in third grade. Her parents had named her Candace, but they called her Candy. Her last name was Hart.

Alanna took the crinkled piece of paper in her hand and crumpled it into a ball, which she shot into her trash can. She didn't need to talk to anyone anyway. She'd get through this the same way she'd gotten through just about everything else in her life. Alone.

"And after that, I think you should write about the long vowel sounds in this line," Melissa said, reaching over Aaron to point at the poem, which lay on the far side of the coffee table. For the first time she'd managed to schedule a study session at her house—when her parents were out to brunch, of course—and it was working out nicely.

She and Aaron were seated side by side on the sofa in the living room, and Melissa had managed to work herself nearer and nearer to him until they were sitting so close, their legs were touching.

"Do you see what I mean?" Melissa asked, tapping the paper. "*O, slow, though*—they're all long *o* sounds, and they really make that line drag. Plus he uses all single-syllable words. You couldn't read that line fast if you wanted to." She flipped her long, brown hair over one shoulder and glanced up at Aaron, still leaning across him.

"Yeah," he said, the warmth of his breath tickling her neck.

Just do it, Melissa willed him, holding his gaze. He stared back at her, his eyes intense with longing, and Melissa thought he might actually be about to kiss her. But just when he seemed ready to move in, he suddenly blinked and looked away instead.

"Um, hey," he started, clearing his throat. "Isn't there a term for that?"

"A term?" Melissa repeated. How could he still be focused on this stupid essay test with her just inches away and totally open to him? What was his problem? What was she doing wrong?

"Yeah. You know—for the vowel sounds," Aaron

said, moving a few inches away and turning on the sofa so that he was facing her. "When you repeat the same ones like that."

"Oh," Melissa said. "Yeah. It's called assonance. And when you repeat consonant sounds, it's called consonance." Aaron quickly scribbled both words down on his note card, obviously planning to use them in his essay, but Melissa wasn't worried. She'd managed to go over the other poem without giving him any terms at all, instead focusing on its meaning and describing some of the literary techniques without actually naming them. So really, it was time she gave him a few to use just to make sure he didn't fail.

"Thanks," Aaron said, glancing up from his writing. "I don't know how you remember all this stuff. You're so smart."

And you're such a coward, Melissa thought. But that was okay. She was going to buy herself enough time to help him work through his bravery issues.

"Thanks," she said. "But really I just have a good memory for useless facts. That's all."

"I don't think so," Aaron said. "You're one of the smartest people I know. And you've really helped me a lot with my English grade."

"Well, just make sure you ace this test tomorrow so that I don't have to give up any more of my free afternoons," Melissa joked.

"I will," Aaron said with a laugh. "Don't worry." He smiled at Melissa for a moment, then looked down at his hands and started fidgeting with his pen. "You know, I'm actually going to miss our study sessions," he said. He glanced up at her and chuckled slightly, but Melissa knew he was serious.

"Me too," she said, making sure to maintain eye contact for a full five seconds so that Aaron would feel the weight of her words. "But hey—at least you'll be able to play in the tournaments without worrying about your English grade anymore."

"Yeah." Aaron nodded. "That's true." Still, even as he smiled, his eyes seemed to droop. But that was okay. Soon enough, he'd understand what Melissa already knew: They still had plenty of time left.

Okay, Andy told himself as he waited for his word-processing program to boot. *This is it.* And when the blank document appeared before him, he was ready.

1. The way Tia just blurts out stuff—like in New York, how she dissed that band on national TV and then found out that they were the guests that day.

2. Evan's constant political ramblings, the way he sees conspiracies everywhere, and you have to be really careful about where you go with him or what kind of food you order when he's around. Your

chicken better be free-range and the produce has to be organic. That kind of stuff.

3. Conner's attitude. Maybe his idea that Disney movies would be better as film noir. Like if Cruella De Vil actually made the jacket.

4. Trent. Big, macho football star who absolutely crumbles around Tia.

5. Jessica and Elizabeth.

Andy was just about to get into the whole identical-twins-with-completely-different-personalities thing when he heard a light knock on his bedroom door.

"Come in," he called.

"How's it going?" his mother asked, poking her head into the room.

"Pretty good, actually," Andy answered. "I mean, I don't have any actual jokes yet, but I've got a lot of stuff to work with."

"That's wonderful," Mrs. Marsden said, beaming. When Andy had told her and his dad that he was planning to try the open-mike thing at the comedy club, they'd both thought it was a great idea. "I just wanted to check in and make sure I'm not the primary source for your material."

Andy laughed. "Of course not," he said.

"Good," Mrs. Marsden replied. "Because comedians always make their mothers out to be either domineering, dumb, or just plain nags, and I don't want to be one of those. Maybe if you use me at all, you can make me out to be some kind of supermom or something. That could be funny, couldn't it?"

"Yeah, sure, Mom," Andy replied, shaking his head at her. Mrs. Marsden grinned, then popped back out and shut the door.

Andy knew she was just kidding. Both of his parents had great senses of humor, which was probably where he had gotten his. And he knew neither one of them would mind what he said about them in a comedy routine—at least not until he made it to *The Tonight Show* or something else with millions of viewers. Then they might start caring. But that wasn't going to happen for a long time, if ever. First he had to get through this open-mike night.

Okay. Where was I? he thought, staring at the computer screen. *Oh, yeah. Jessica and Elizabeth.* He had poised his hands above the keyboard, ready to start in again, when a thought occurred to him.

Sure, his parents had great senses of humor, and they wouldn't care what he said about them, but they were his parents. How were his friends going to feel if they found out that his entire comedy routine was based on them?

They'd laugh, Andy told himself, getting ready to type again. But somehow, even though his fingers were ready, his mind wasn't. His thoughts weren't flowing quite so freely now.

Oh, come on, he told himself. *You're just going to do a few jokes. Nobody's going to care.* But even as he repeated those thoughts over and over to himself, he wasn't entirely convinced his friends would find a comedy routine focused on their shortcomings all that funny. *They might laugh. Eventually,* Andy told himself. But he wasn't sure if the laughter would come before or after they had stopped speaking to him. Probably after.

He grabbed the mouse and highlighted the text he had just written, staring at it. There was some good stuff there—stuff he could turn into a decent routine. The question was, could he, in good conscience, get up onstage and goof on his friends, knowing that it might upset them?

Andy took a deep breath and hit the delete button. The answer was no. A few good jokes weren't important enough to risk a lot of good friendships. He'd just have to come up with different material. But what?

Andy Marsden

Let's see. Everyone loves a good chicken joke, right?

1. Why did the chicken cross the playground? To get to the other slide.
2. What disease do chickens get in the winter? Influ-<u>hen</u>-za.
3. What do you call a chicken's laugh? A cluckle.

Okay, maybe not. But how about pigs? Pigs are funny. Aren't they?

Oh, boy. From friends to farm animals. I'm doomed.

CHAPTER 4

Break a Leg . . . or Something

Andy shifted his weight from his left foot to his right and back again. He was trying not to let his nerves get the best of him, but it was hard to stay calm while standing in line for open-mike night at a packed comedy club.

The guy who was onstage now was doing okay. His jokes were pretty good—some stuff about his dog, his boss, his girlfriend—and the audience seemed pretty receptive, even though there was still an undercurrent of conversation going on.

Mostly the chatter was coming from the bar area, which was in a section of the club Andy hadn't even noticed the last time he'd been here. When he and Dave had come before, they'd sat at the back, so Andy hadn't seen the seating area upstairs. But from where he was standing now—at the front of the room, just to the right of the stage—he could see it clearly, and the club looked completely different.

The upstairs was like a wide balcony overlooking

the stage, and the bar was at the back. There were people sitting on bar stools and at tables and even some just standing, balancing their drinks on the wooden rail. Andy guessed that in addition to the twenty-five to thirty tables on the first floor, there were probably ten to fifteen upstairs, along with the bar stools and standing room. *That means this club can fit . . .* Andy made an attempt at the math and gave up. *Well, a lot more people than I thought.* And tonight it seemed to be pretty full.

Realizing that staring at the crowd wasn't doing much for his nerves, Andy turned his attention back to the stage. This guy had been out there for nearly five minutes now, which was about how long people usually stayed, so Andy knew he was almost done. And that meant it was almost Andy's turn. It was a thought that filled him with both excitement and terror, but before he could dwell on either emotion, the emcee stood up, signaling that it was time for the next act.

"I'm Joe Hallett—thanks a lot," the man onstage said with a wave. There was mild applause as he walked off, but nothing special. In fact, the people on the upper level didn't even seem to realize he had finished. Andy couldn't help thinking it was kind of rude of them not to clap—the guy hadn't been half bad. But he decided it just meant that he was going to have to be better. And he could do it. He knew he could.

"Thank you, Joe," the emcee said, clapping and turning toward the audience, encouraging them to do the same. A few people obliged him. When the sprinkling of applause died down, he placed one hand on the mike stand. "For those of you who arrived late, welcome to Sierra's Open Mike Night. We have a lot of talent here for you tonight, including our next act."

Andy's heart began to pound. This was it. He was up.

"This young man is a high-school senior, and he's here tonight to take his first shot at the microphone. So please, put your hands together and join me in welcoming Mr. Andy Marsden."

Again the emcee clapped at the audience as if he were leading them in a giant game of Simon says. And even though he hadn't said the magic words, most of the people on the first floor clapped along with him.

"Um, thanks," Andy said as the applause died down. "But actually, this is my second shot at the microphone. My first was in New York." Andy waited, expecting at least one person in the audience to applaud or whistle. They always did that on TV, no matter what city was named, but it was silent. Except, of course, for the noise coming from upstairs.

"So, then, I guess there aren't any New Yorkers in the crowd tonight, huh?" he said. Again there was no response. "Because, you know, no one . . . clapped or anything."

The white lights above the stage beat down on him, making it hard to see the audience. Even so, Andy was fairly certain no one was shaking with silent laughter.

Think, Marsden, think, he admonished himself. But every joke he'd ever heard—including the ones he'd considered telling tonight—seemed to have vanished from his head. And now, to make matters even worse, he was beginning to sweat. The heat from the lights was much more intense here than he remembered it being in New York.

New York, he thought. *That's it. If I could just remember some of the material I used there.*

"Um, so anyway, when I was in New York, I noticed that just about everyone there was dressed in black. It was like the whole city was inhabited by creatures of the night, you know?" Two women who were sitting at a table in the front squinted up at him, and Andy ran a hand through his mop of red hair, trying to remember what had been so funny about that before. "Black turtlenecks," he added suddenly. "They were all wearing black *turtlenecks.* Like, to hide the bite marks, you know."

Oh, crap, Andy thought. *Maybe they didn't get it. . . . Should I add something in about vampires? No, that'll just make it worse.*

71

"Oh—and they all smoked too," he went on. "Not like here, in sunny California, where everyone has replaced their nicotine habits with tofu and yoga."

Andy watched as the few people who had still been paying attention began whispering to their friends or digging into their appetizers. Oh, boy. This wasn't going well at all.

"We're such a healthy state, you know? I mean, I don't think I've even seen anyone out here wearing a patch, but maybe that's just because no one's been able to manufacture one that doesn't leave tan lines yet." Andy thought he heard one person in the back chuckle, and he was almost encouraged to go on. But then, before he had a real chance to salvage himself, he saw the emcee approaching.

"Let's have a big hand for Mr. Andy Marsden," he called, modeling applause for the audience once again. Andy winced and started off the stage, not even bothering to say thank you or wave or anything. There was a decent volume of clapping, but Andy knew he hadn't earned it. People were only applauding out of pity.

I can't believe it. I tanked, he told himself. That was the term he'd always heard comedians use for being pulled offstage before their acts were done, but he'd never thought he'd be using it himself.

He walked down the stairs and started toward the

back of the club, staring at the floor all the way. He was so embarrassed that he didn't want to make eye contact with anyone. He didn't even want to stick around to hear any of the other acts. He just wanted to get out of there as fast as possible.

But just as he reached the door and got ready to push it open, an older man stepped over and put his hand on Andy's shoulder. "You've got talent, kid," he said, patting Andy on the back a couple of times.

"Yeah, right. I was great up there," Andy said, his voice flat.

"That's not what I said," the man replied, holding up his index finger. "I said you've got talent." He gestured back toward the stage. "You were horrible up there, and we both know it."

Andy widened his eyes. He *had* been horrible, and he *did* know it, but that didn't mean he wanted other people pointing it out to him. Especially not some old, bald guy who was blocking his exit.

"Hey—I'm just telling you the truth, kid," the man continued. "You bombed tonight—but that doesn't mean you're gonna bomb next time. You have a great look," he said, nodding toward Andy's hair, "and a good voice. And you've got great timing. You just need some decent material."

"Uh, thanks," Andy said, though he wasn't buying a word of it.

"I just tell it like it is," the guy said. "And trust me—I know what I'm talking about. So you come back another night and try again. You'll do a lot better next time."

"It would be hard to do worse," Andy said, "but still—I don't think there's going to be a next time."

"Sure, there is," the guy said, clapping Andy on the back again. "Just remember these two things. Number one," he started, holding up one chubby finger, "have a few jokes ready in advance. Practice them in front of a mirror and say them a thousand times before you come so you'll have something to fall back on if you draw a blank. Got it?"

Andy nodded, though he was still wondering who on earth this guy was.

"And number two: Stick with what you know. Your family, your friends, your job—or, in your case, school. Those are the two rules of comedy, kid. Master them and you'll be on your way. All right?"

"S-sure," Andy said, and the bald guy clapped him on the back again. But at least he was finished. He'd already turned back toward the stage and started watching the next act.

Phew, that was weird, Andy thought as he made his way across the parking lot to his mother's minivan. He wondered if the bald guy just stood there all night, stopping everybody on their way out and giving them all the same advice. *Probably. What a freak.* Even so, there was some truth in what he'd said, and Andy knew it.

It probably was a good idea to practice in advance and have a couple of jokes to fall back on—especially when you were just starting out. In fact, now that he thought about it, he remembered Maria saying that lots of stage actors had stock lines they used whenever they forgot what they were really supposed to be saying. It was a way of buying themselves time to remember their real lines instead of standing there in an awkward silence.

And the other thing he'd said made sense too. Stick to what you know—your friends, your family, school. Those *were* the things that were funny—little observations about the people and places you really knew well. But that was the problem.

If Andy went up onstage and made fun of the people he knew, he wouldn't know them much longer. And keeping his friends was definitely more important than being funny.

Especially since—as he'd found out tonight—he wasn't.

Alanna clicked the send-and-receive button on her e-mail program and waited. No new messages. Just like there hadn't been any new messages when she'd checked five minutes ago.

She glanced over at her nightstand, where her copy of *Othello* was sitting, and grimaced. Sooner or later she was going to have get back to her homework. She would have preferred it to be later, but since no one was e-mailing or calling or stopping by to help her procrastinate, it looked like it was going to be sooner.

She tried checking for e-mail one more time, but there was nothing. "Fine," she muttered, trudging across the floor. "You win, Shakespeare." But just as she was about to flop down on her bed and start reading, the phone rang.

"*Yes,*" she whispered, dropping the book and picking up the phone. "Hello?"

"Hello, this is Sandra Bietche. Could I please speak with Alanna?"

"Uh . . . well," Alanna started. *Sandra. Shoot. Why is she calling me?* Alanna was desperate to avoid her homework, but not that desperate. A conversation about alcoholism or her fight with her dad was just about the last thing she needed right now. Besides, a whole day had passed. She was doing a lot better now. "Um, she's not home. Can I take a message?"

There was a pause. "Is *this* Alanna?"

"Uh—uh . . . no," Alanna stammered. "Why?"

"It's okay, you know. I hung up on my sponsor the first time I called too. Don't worry about it."

Alanna considered pressing on with her lie and pretending to be a maid or something, but there didn't seem to be any point. "How did you know I called?" she asked.

"I got your name and number off my caller-ID box," Sandra explained. "And I knew right away who you were. Alanna is my sister's name too. I remembered thinking it was a coincidence when the A.A. facilitator gave me your name and asked me to serve as your interim sponsor. It's not a very common name, so I guess it stuck."

"No, I guess it's not," Alanna said. "But then again, neither is yours."

"Oh, God. Isn't it terrible?" Sandra asked. "I can't imagine what my parents were thinking when they named me. *Sandy Bietche*. And we live in California—the land of sandy beaches. Oh, well. At least you didn't think it was pronounced 'bitch.' I get that a lot too."

"No way," Alanna said, laughing. "There's an *e* at the end."

"Well, telemarketers do it to me all the time. They're probably just taking out all their anger on me. If I had people hanging up on me all day, I'd be angry too. You know, I'm all for women keeping their last names when they get married—I think it's cool. But I tell you, the minute I get engaged, I'm filling out the forms. I can't wait to drop Bietche and get something new. I'd even settle for Smith—or Jones. Or Brown. Something simple, you know?"

Alanna giggled, surprised at just how funny Sandra seemed to be. For some reason, she'd expected her A.A. sponsor to be some stodgy, puritanical woman who warned her about the evils of "the drink."

"But that's enough about my name problems. So what's up with you?"

Alanna bit her lip. "Oh, it's nothing, really. I just had a bad day yesterday. That's all."

"A bad day can be a big deal," Sandra said. "Especially when you're an alcoholic. How are you doing now?"

Alanna wrinkled her nose. "Okay, I guess."

"Are you feeling the urge to take a drink or anything?" Sandra asked.

"Oh. No. I wasn't even doing that bad yesterday," Alanna assured her. She didn't want Sandra to think she was totally unstable or anything. "I was just really angry, and I needed to vent."

"Well, then, you know what?"

"What?" Alanna asked.

"You should. But since it's not an emergency—I mean, since you've had a whole day to calm down— why don't we do it over coffee instead of over the phone? You can vent, and I'll complain about my name some more."

"Um, okay," Alanna agreed with a giggle. "When?"

"How about right now?"

Alanna glanced at her *Othello* book. It wasn't like she had anything better to do. "Sure. Where do you want to meet?"

"There's a place just around the corner from where I work called Still Life with Coffee—do you know it?"

"Yeah, it's pretty close to my house, actually—only about ten minutes away."

"Great. Then I'll meet you there in a half hour, okay?"

"Okay," Alanna agreed, and she hung up the phone.

It was strange to think that in fifteen minutes she'd be meeting her A.A. sponsor face-to-face when just five minutes ago she'd been trying to lie her way out of speaking to her on the phone. But Sandra seemed cool, and she definitely had a good sense of humor. So maybe this sponsor thing wouldn't be so bad.

At the very least, Alanna would have someone to talk to—a second option for when Conner gave her bad advice like, "Don't take it so personally." But even more important, meeting with Sandra gave her a good reason to avoid Shakespeare for another hour or so. Yup, this sponsor thing was working out already.

*   *   *

"Which tie?" Dave asked, holding two up against his chest in turn.

Andy, who was sitting on Dave's living-room floor flipping through old comic books, glanced up and squinted. "I'm not the person to ask," he said. "Tia dresses me."

"Well, then," Dave said, chuckling, "which one would Tia pick?"

Andy furrowed his brow and scrutinized Dave's outfit. Navy suit, white oxford shirt. "The green one," he said. "No, wait—that's what I'd wear. Tia would choose that blue one with the orange squares."

"Orange squares it is," Dave said. He draped the green tie over the back of the couch and went out into the hall, where there was a full-length mirror, to knot his tie. "I'm sorry I can't hang out," he called. "I just found out about this banquet today, and I really want to be there to accept the scholarship."

"No problem," Andy said.

"I wish you could come," Dave said. "But they only gave me two tickets—one for me and one for my dad. I guess it's a big dinner thing, and scholarship winners from a lot of other schools are going to be there too."

"Sounds cool," Andy said, going back to his comic book. Maybe someday he'd get invited to a banquet. *Yeah, sure. Only if I'm the one hosting it,* he thought.

"Are you okay, Andy?" Dave asked, poking his head into the room. "You sound a little down."

Andy shrugged. "Nah, I'm fine. Just tired, I guess." He hadn't bothered to tell Dave about the comedy club, even though that had been his original reason for stopping by after school.

"Are you sure?"

"Yeah," Andy insisted.

Dave finished with his tie and stepped back into the living room. "So," he began, "have you thought any more about going to one of those open-mike nights at Sierra's?"

Andy closed his eyes and sighed. He really didn't want to get into it now—not when Dave had a banquet to go to—but he wasn't going to lie.

"Yeah. Actually, I went to one last night."

"You did? That's awesome! How did it go?"

"Not so awesome," Andy admitted.

Dave took a seat on the sofa opposite Andy. "That's too bad," he said. "What happened?"

"I totally bombed," Andy said. "I got pulled off-stage before I even got started. It was pathetic."

"Come on. I'm sure it wasn't that bad," Dave said.

Andy stared directly into his eyes without blinking. "Worse," he said. He walked over to the sofa and plunked himself down next to Dave, leaning back and folding his arms across his chest.

Dave shook his head. "But you're so funny," he protested. "What went wrong? Were you nervous?"

Andy shrugged. "Not really. I mean, a little, maybe, but that wasn't the problem."

"So what was?"

"I just didn't have anything to say. Some guy at the door nailed me on it. He told me I should have at least a few things prepared in advance—to fall back on."

"That makes sense," Dave said.

"Yeah, but he also said I should stick with what I know. Friends, family, that kind of stuff. And I can't do that."

"Why not?"

"Because," Andy said. It seemed obvious to him, but Dave was giving him a blank stare. "How would people like it if I got up there and started talking about them?"

"They wouldn't care," Dave said with a shrug. "That's what comedians do."

Andy cocked his head. "Are you serious?"

"Yeah. Why?"

"I don't know," Andy said. "I just figured everyone would get upset with me if I started making fun of them onstage."

"Like who?" Dave asked. "Tia? She wouldn't mind. She's got a great sense of humor. Trent? He thinks you're hilarious. They'd probably love it if you used them in your act."

Andy leaned forward. "You think so?"

"Sure. When are you going to do it again?"

"I'm not," Andy said.

"Oh, come on—you have to."

"I don't know," Andy said. "I mean, I'd have to come up with some material first." Of course, if he really could use his friends, coming up with ideas wouldn't be all that hard. It had certainly come easily enough when he'd sat down to type yesterday. But still . . . how could he be sure no one was going to get upset?

"Do you really think people would be okay with me using them in my routine?" he pressed.

"Of course they would," Dave said. "They're big boys and girls—they can handle it."

Andy bit his lip. He wished he could be as certain about it as Dave. And the bald guy.

"Besides," Dave continued, "it's way too soon for you to give up. You've only given it one shot. Do you know how many scholarships I applied for?" Andy shook his head. "Twenty-two," Dave said. "And so far I've only gotten one."

Andy raised his eyebrows. Twenty-two was way more than he'd imagined. He'd figured that Dave had just got the first one he'd tried for. Maybe Dave was right. Perseverance was the name of the game.

Besides, all artists drew material from their own lives, right? Writers, painters, singers, comedians—they all did it. And besides, if he just kept moping around and acting upset and bored by everything, his friends were going to get sick of him anyway. Whether he made fun of them or not.

Melissa Fox

Okay, so I kind of sabotaged Aaron. But it's not like one bad grade is really going to hurt him. He'll still have his B average in time for the tournaments—or at least he should. But even if he doesn't, it won't be my fault. After all, he was <u>failing</u> English before I started helping him. At least now he's passing.

Besides, I'm not the one who put Aaron in the middle of everything. Will and Cherie did when they turned their backs on me. All I'm doing is defending myself and letting them know that they can't treat me that way. And soon enough, they'll understand that.

CHAPTER
A Successful Failure
5

"Hey, Cherie, wait up," Melissa called, jogging after her friend.

Cherie stopped just outside the locker-room door and let Melissa catch up. "What's going on?"

"I was just wondering if you wanted to grab a postpractice frozen yogurt and catch up. We haven't had a chance to hang out for a while." *And I need to find out what's going on between you and Aaron,* Melissa thought. If Cherie was the reason Aaron wasn't making a move, she wanted to know.

"Oh. Thanks," Cherie said. "But I'm not really in the mood." She opened the locker-room door and started in, holding it for Melissa.

"Really? Why not?" Melissa asked.

"I don't know," Cherie said, setting her pompoms down on one of the benches and turning to open her locker. "I just don't feel like going out. I have a lot of homework to do."

"Homework can wait," Melissa told her. "Besides, I'm buying."

Cherie turned her head toward Melissa and gave her a weak smile. "Thanks, but I'm just not up for it." She fumbled with her lock, then swung open her door and began pulling out her duffel bag. But as soon as she had it halfway out of the locker, everything else started tumbling down too.

"This is *not* my day," Cherie said, stooping to pick up her sneakers, her shampoo, and everything else that had landed in a heap on the floor.

Melissa leaned down to help her, scooping up as many things as she could and setting them on the bench.

"Thanks," Cherie said.

"No problem," Melissa replied. "So . . . what's going on? I have a feeling there's something besides homework keeping you from coming to the Gazebo with me."

Cherie slumped down on the bench. "Yeah," she said. She glanced around at the other cheerleaders, who were still gathering their things. Most of them were either already gone or in the showers, but there were a few girls talking on the other side of the lockers, and it was obvious Cherie didn't want anyone to overhear what she was about to say.

Melissa took a seat next to her on the bench and waited.

"It's Aaron," Cherie said finally, keeping her voice low.

"What about him?" Melissa asked.

Cherie shook her head. "I don't know. It's like he's totally lost interest in me, but I don't know why."

Melissa felt a fluttering sensation in her stomach and had to resist the urge to smile. Instead she clicked her tongue. "I'm sure that's not true. I've been talking you up to him nonstop, and he always seems happy to listen. What makes you think he's not interested?"

"Well, it used to be that when I called him or talked to him at his locker, he seemed really interested, you know?" Melissa nodded. "It was, like, I just got a good vibe from him, and he always asked me questions about stuff like he wanted to know more about me."

"So what's changed?" Melissa asked.

Cherie sighed. "Last night when I called him, I barely got three words out before he said he had a lot of homework to do and couldn't talk. And then today, when I went over to his locker after lunch, he talked to me for a second, but I don't think he ever even looked at me. It was like he had something else on his mind and I was interrupting. And then he said he didn't want to be late for class and took off."

"Is that it?" Melissa asked.

Cherie nodded. "I just don't think he's interested in me."

"Don't be ridiculous," Melissa told her. "Just because he's been a little distant for two days, that doesn't mean anything."

"But it's been more than two days," Cherie said. "It's like he's been distracted every time I've talked to him for at least a week now—maybe longer."

"Hmmm," Melissa murmured. It definitely didn't sound like Aaron's feelings for Cherie were what was holding him back, and she was relieved to hear it. But if that wasn't the problem, what was?

"So what do you think?" Cherie asked after a minute. "Have I totally blown it or what?"

Melissa shook her head. "I don't think so," she said. "You know, Aaron had a really big English test today, and if he gets a good grade on it, he'll be all set for the rest of basketball season. I bet that's why he's been so distracted."

"Do you really think so?" Cherie asked, straightening up.

"Yeah. I do," Melissa said. "You know how important basketball is to him. I'm sure that test is really weighing on his mind."

"Wow. I hadn't thought of that. I didn't even know he had one today—that's how little he's been talking to me lately."

"Well, I'm sure that's what it is," Melissa told her. "And I'm willing to bet that if you just give him a little space until after he finds out how he did, everything will fall right back into place for you."

Cherie grabbed Melissa's hands and squeezed them. "Oh, I hope you're right," she said, flashing Melissa a big smile.

"Of course I'm right. Now, how about some ice cream?"

"You're on," Cherie said. She stood up and started packing her things into her duffel bag. "I'm just going to shower at home," she said, throwing in her towel as well.

"Me too," said Melissa. "Let's go." She grabbed her backpack and slammed her locker shut, and Cherie did the same. As they started out the door, Cherie stopped and turned to her.

"Thanks, Melissa. You must be so sick of hearing me whine about Aaron."

"Not at all. That's what friends are for," Melissa replied. "Right?"

"Right," Cherie agreed. "And you really think I still have a shot with Aaron?"

"Absolutely," Melissa lied. "Especially once this essay test is out of the way. I'm sure you'll have much better luck with him once he gets his grade." *Or at least one of us will.*

*　　　*　　　*

When Alanna walked into Still Life with Coffee, she immediately understood where it had gotten its name. The burgundy walls were decorated with frames of various sizes and shapes, all featuring artwork done by numerous artists in different mediums.

There was a pastel chalk drawing of an orchid in a thin, glass vase near the coffee bar, and next to it, an oil painting of three cows in the middle of a field. Each picture had its name below it, along with the name of the artist, a brief description, and a price. Alanna took a step toward the cows to get a closer look and discovered that it was priced at 750 dollars.

"Whew," Alanna whistled, shaking her head.

"A bit much for a five by seven of some cows grazing, don't you think?" a voice behind her asked. Alanna whirled around to see a woman with short, black hair sticking out from under a knit cap. She had bright blue eyes and a friendly smile, and Alanna knew it had to be Sandra.

"Alanna, right?" the woman said, extending her hand.

"Yeah." Alanna nodded. "Sandra?"

"You got it," she replied as they shook hands. "Have you ordered anything yet?" Sandra asked, gesturing toward the counter.

"No, I just got here," Alanna said.

"Good. Let me get you something, then," Sandra offered, walking up to the counter.

"Oh, you don't have to," Alanna said, following her, but Sandra just waved her hand.

"I'll have a mochaccino with whipped cream and grated chocolate, please," Sandra started, "and she'll have . . ." She pointed to Alanna.

"Um, a small coffee," Alanna said. "But really, Sandra, you don't have to—"

"You can pay next time," Sandra told her, handing the cashier a ten.

"All right," Alanna agreed. She took the white mug the cashier handed her and went over to the self-serve island, where she filled it with the house decaf, some cream, and one spoonful of sugar. By the time she'd finished stirring it all together, Sandra's drink was ready, so together they walked to a table near one of the back windows and sat down.

"This is a cool place," Alanna said, gazing around at all of the artwork on the walls.

"Mmmm," Sandra agreed, taking a sip of her mochaccino. A layer of cream coated her upped lip, but she just laughed and wiped it off with her napkin. "I work right around the corner, but I try not to come in too much. Between the chocolate and the cream I could get seriously fat on these things."

Alanna laughed, noting Sandra's slim figure. "I don't think you need to worry," she said.

"That's because I don't come in too much,"

Sandra replied, shaking a finger. She glanced around the room. "In fact, I think most of this artwork is new since the last time I was in about a month ago."

"Wow, you really don't come here much," Alanna said. She glanced to her left, where a painting at the other side of the room had caught her attention. It was a rowboat set adrift in the middle of a lake, its reflection shimmering on the dark water. The trees at the far side of the lake were reflected as well, and the whole scene seemed incredibly peaceful. Alanna found herself wishing she could crawl into the boat and lie down, just for a few minutes. It would be so quiet, she could tell, with only the sound of branches rustling in the breeze and small waves lapping the side of the boat.

"I like that one too," Sandra said.

"Huh? Oh, sorry," Alanna apologized. "I guess I was sort of daydreaming."

"I can see why," Sandra said, staring over at the painting. "It looks so calm, and I love the color of the water. It's almost black, but there are hints of blue and green. And the way it's kind of cloudy reminds me of Monet's water lilies."

"Those are my favorite paintings," Alanna said, wondering when Sandra was going to bring up the A.A. stuff. She cleared her throat and shuffled in her chair. "Well, that and just about anything by Renoir. I love impressionism."

"Then you should definitely check out the exhibit at the de Young Memorial Museum in San Francisco," Sandra said. "I don't know how much longer it runs, but they have a bunch of impressionists there now. And actually, I think they have quite a few in their permanent collection as well."

Maybe Sandra just wants to shoot the breeze this time.

"Really? I'll have to try to get up there," Alanna said. She took a sip of her decaf and watched Sandra, who was still looking at the painting. She was wearing a pair of really cool, dangly, silver earrings with amethysts at the bottom that bobbed against her long, elegant neck. Her jet-black hair was cut at a sharp angle just below her earlobes, and there was an almost bluish tint to it. Alanna placed her at thirty-three, maybe thirty-five, tops.

"You should," Sandra said, turning back to her. "And so should I. Maybe we can take a day trip sometime." Alanna brightened. Somehow she already knew she'd enjoy hanging out with Sandra. The two of them just seemed to click. "But do you know what we should do right now?"

"What?" *Uh-oh. Here it comes. . . .*

"Talk about what was bugging you so much yesterday before I have to get back to work," Sandra said, and Alanna slumped in her seat. She'd been having such a good time talking with Sandra that she'd almost forgotten why they were here. "So what's up?"

Alanna heaved a sigh, but she knew she was going to have talk about it sooner or later, if only to get some better advice than what Conner had given her.

"Nothing, really," she said. "I mean, it's not a big deal. I just had a fight with my father."

"What about?" Sandra asked, takng a sip of her mochaccino.

"Well . . . I was supposed to write this letter—sort of a thank-you note—to some friends of my parents, and I kind of told him that I'd already done it when I hadn't." Sandra nodded, encouraging Alanna to continue. "So anyway, my dad found the envelope and realized that I hadn't actually done it yet, and he got all bent out of shape."

"What did he say?" Sandra asked.

"A lot of stuff," Alanna said, realizing that some of the things he'd said were still bothering her—at least enough that she didn't feel like repeating it all.

"And you were pretty upset, huh?"

"Oh, yeah," Alanna agreed. "And to make it even worse, I—"

"You what?" Sandra asked.

"I . . . couldn't think of anyone to call," Alanna lied. She didn't want to bring Conner into the mix—at least not yet.

"But you called me," Sandra said, "and that's

good. It means you were ready and willing to ask for help when you needed it—and if you keep on doing that, you're much less likely to turn to alcohol as a solution to your problems, right?"

"Right," Alanna said.

"But this thing with your father is really bothering you, isn't it?"

"Yeah, I guess so," Alanna agreed. "I just wish there was some way to make him understand how hard all this is for me. He makes it sound like I'm just goofing around—like if I wanted to straighten everything out, I could just snap my fingers or something and turn into the perfect daughter."

"That's hard," Sandra agreed, "and I wish there was some kind of magic answer I could give you, but the truth is, he might never completely understand what you're going through. People who haven't experienced alcoholism don't always comprehend it very well, and it is a hard thing to deal with."

"So there's no way to change things with my parents, then," Alanna said, gazing into her coffee cup. She could see the shape of her head—curly hair sticking out all over—reflected in the light brown liquid.

"That's not what I said," Sandra corrected her. "I said your dad might never understand alcoholism as completely as you want him to, but that doesn't mean you have to stop trying to talk to him about it. What you *do* have to do, though, is stop taking his comments so personally."

Alanna screwed up her face. "I can't believe it. That's exactly . . ." She paused and took a sip of her coffee, stalling for time. "That's exactly what I thought, at first. But it's so hard to do."

Sandra stared at her sideways for a second, but she didn't comment on Alanna's near slip. "It is hard to do," she agreed, "especially when you're dealing with your parents. But you have to remember that they're human—they're going to blurt out things that they don't mean too. So you can't take every little comment they make personally. If you do, you're going to drive yourself crazy."

Isn't that the truth, Alanna thought, but she was still a bit surprised that Sandra had given her exactly the same advice as Conner had.

"Hey—I hope that helps a little," Sandra said. "Unfortunately, I have to get back to work. But maybe we should do this again sometime, maybe later in the day so that I won't have to rush off," she suggested.

"Yeah, I'd like that," Alanna agreed.

"And in the meantime, call whenever you need to."

"Thanks."

Sandra stood to go, then turned to Alanna. "Just out of curiosity, what kind of support system do you have? You know—who else can you talk to? Your mom? A friend? Anyone?"

"Um . . . well," Alanna started. It still seemed too early to bring up Conner. "There's my friend, Lisa. But she's in Chicago."

"Anyone else?" Sandra asked.

Alanna shook her head. "No, not really," she said, staring into her coffee.

"Well, you've got me," Sandra said. "And you've got all the other people at A.A. too—so you're not alone."

"Yeah." Alanna nodded. "I know."

Sandra sat back down and reached across the table, touching Alanna's hand lightly. "Alcoholism can be a really isolating disease," she said. "I was pretty much alone when I started getting sober too. But over time, as I've gotten stronger on my own, I've been able to rebuild some old relationships— like with my family—and start some new ones too."

Alanna blinked rapidly, still focusing on her coffee mug. It was strange how easily the tears came whenever someone was genuinely kind to her.

"It will get better," Sandra told her. "Really, it will. And in a way, it's kind of a good thing that you're not in a relationship right now."

Alanna raised her head. "It is?"

"Yeah," Sandra said, smiling. "I know it sounds weird, but you're actually kind of lucky."

"Lucky?" Alanna echoed, screwing up her face. "Why?"

"Because relationships can get messy—especially when you're trying to get your life in order."

"Yeah, but . . . wouldn't it be good if I had someone I could talk to? Someone who really understood me?"

"Sure." Sandra nodded. "But it doesn't have to be a boyfriend. You can get that kind of support from a friend—or even from your A.A. sponsor," she added, giving Alanna's hand a squeeze.

"I guess," Alanna said.

"And that way you don't have to deal with any of the pressure that comes with a relationship—you can really focus on yourself. And on getting healthy and sober. Then when you *do* meet someone, you'll be in a much better place for it."

Alanna nodded to let Sandra know she was still listening, but she wasn't sure she agreed with anything Sandra was saying. The place she was in right now—with Conner—was a good one. She couldn't imagine anything better.

"Yeah, if I were you," Sandra continued, "I'd wait as long as you can to start dating."

"You would?"

"Mm-hmm," Sandra replied. "You're young—you've got plenty of time for all of that. Right now you should concentrate on *you*. That's the most important thing."

Sandra smiled warmly, and Alanna forced herself to smile back. After all, Sandra was just looking out for Alanna's best interests. Still, Alanna was glad she'd kept her mouth shut about Conner.

Maybe there wasn't a rule about dating in the first year or anything. But Sandra was the second person in two days to suggest that getting involved with someone while you were trying to get sober wasn't exactly smart.

"Thank you for coming down here to meet me," Sandra said, standing up. "I'm glad you admitted it was really you on the phone."

"Yeah, me too."

"Oh—I almost forgot," Sandra said, reaching into her bag. "I brought along a couple of work sheets someone gave me when I first joined A.A. You can do whatever you want with them—read them, fill them out, don't fill them out—it's up to you. I just thought you might find them helpful."

She handed Alanna a packet of papers neatly clipped together. "Thanks," Alanna said.

"You're welcome—take care. And I'm sure I'll see you at one of the upcoming meetings—I usually try to make the Thursday nights on a regular basis. This week I might try to make Wednesday as well."

"Cool. Maybe I'll see you there," Alanna said.

When Sandra had gone, Alanna took a sip of her coffee and started to flip through the work sheets, but then she had a better idea. She pulled her cell phone out of her pocketbook instead.

"Hello?"

"Hi, Conner, this is Alanna."

"Hey, I—"

"Wait. Before you say anything, I need to apologize. You were right about my father. I need to stop taking everything he says so personally, and I never should have gotten so angry at you for saying so. I'm really sorry." She waited a minute, but there was silence at the other end. "Conner? Are you still there?"

"Yeah, sorry. I just—are you okay?" he asked.

"I'm fine," Alanna said. "I've just been thinking a lot about what you said the other day, and I decided it was actually good advice."

"You did?"

"Yes—so, thank you. And I really am sorry."

"Don't worry about it," Conner said. Alanna closed her eyes and smiled. Things were so easy with Conner—so comfortable and natural. Maybe other people needed to wait a year to start dating, but she couldn't imagine going a single day without Conner.

"You know," Conner said. "I've been thinking too."

"You have?"

"Yeah. I think I'm going to go to the A.A. meetings on a regular basis again."

"Really?"

"Yeah. Just to keep myself on track. Wanna join me?" he suggested.

Alanna winced. She hated going to the meetings, but she knew Conner was right. The last few weeks had been a little rough for both of them—especially her.

"Yeah," she agreed. "I probably should."

"So what do you think? Your meeting site or mine?"

My meeting site? Alanna thought. *No way.* She wasn't about to introduce Conner to Sandra—that would be way too risky. For one thing, if Sandra found out that Alanna had a boyfriend, she'd realize Alanna had lied to her—in the first twenty minutes of knowing her. Plus after everything Sandra had said about dating, she'd probably encourage Alanna to put the relationship on hold, and that was something Alanna wasn't willing to do.

"You know what?" Alanna said. "I think maybe we should go to separate meeting sites. You know, you go to yours, I'll go to mine."

"Why?"

"I don't know. It just seems like maybe we'd get more out of it that way. You know, without each other there as a distraction."

"You don't distract me," Conner said, sounding like he was smiling.

How can I say no when he's being so cute? Alanna thought. But she didn't know how to juggle everything.

If she wanted to hang out with Sandra—which she did—she needed to go to her local meetings. But if Conner came too, Sandra would know she had lied, and then her opinion of Alanna was sure to plummet.

It was weird. Even though she'd just met Sandra, she already felt close to her. It was like having a big sister all of a sudden, and Alanna didn't want to risk losing her.

"Well, I think I'd like to try going alone for a while," Alanna said. "Just to see."

"All right," Conner said. "Whatever."

"Good." Alanna heaved a sigh of relief. She'd managed to dodge that one pretty easily. Now if she could just get herself to attend a meeting alone. *But I won't be alone,* she told herself. *Sandra will be there.* And that was a comforting thought.

When Melissa got out of English, she made a point of rushing down the hall so that she would be just outside Aaron's class as he and Will exited. They were supposed to get their essays back today, and Melissa was dying to see if her plan had worked.

She parked herself across the hall from O'Reilly's room just in time to see Will coming out, with Aaron close behind. Will noticed her immediately and started walking toward her. Aaron followed automatically, but when he caught sight of Melissa, his pace slowed down and his eyes shifted toward his feet.

"How did you do?" Melissa asked as Will approached.

"Ninety-two," Will said. Melissa smiled and nodded at him, but Aaron was the one she was really concerned about.

"And how about you?" she asked, stretching a hopeful grin across her face.

Aaron kicked at the floor with the toe of his sneaker a few times, then slowly looked up. "Eighty-one," he said. "B-minus."

Melissa dropped her jaw and let out an indignant huff. "What? How did that happen? We worked so hard on your outline." Aaron shrugged and went back to staring at his shoes.

"Let me look at that," Melissa said, grabbing paper out of his hand. "I don't believe it," she said, flipping through the three-page essay Aaron had written and noting the lack of red check marks. There were a few, but not many. Aaron had only used the terms Melissa had given him. "Is this the way she always grades? Just checking off terms?"

"You know it is, Liss," Will cut in. "I've been complaining about O'Reilly all—"

"Why aren't there any comments or anything?" Melissa interrupted. "You have all the right information in here. She should have given you a much higher grade."

"Yeah, well, I guess she didn't think so," Aaron mumbled.

"Oh, Aaron. I'm so sorry," Melissa said. "If only I'd known that she was just going to look for buzz-words, I would have gone about this essay in a completely different way."

"You *did* know, Liss," Will said. "I've been complaining about O'Reilly's glance-and-grade system for months now."

"Was it English you were complaining about?" Melissa said, screwing up her face. "For some reason I thought it was history class." She shook her head. "Either way, I obviously messed up. But that's okay," she said, handing Aaron back his paper. "It just means we're going to have to work twice as hard over the next week to improve your grade—and I'm sure we can do it."

At that, Aaron brightened, a smile spreading across his face, but Melissa couldn't help noticing that Will didn't exactly look thrilled.

"I got a ninety-two on the test," Will said. "Maybe *I* should tutor Aaron."

Melissa laughed. "Oh, sure, when? On your way to the *Tribune*? I don't think so. You hardly have time for your own homework."

"I have plenty of time," Will said, glaring at Melissa.

"Hey, I appreciate the offer, man," Aaron said,

patting Will's shoulder. "But I know how busy you are, and I wouldn't want to cut into your internship. Besides, Melissa and I have already established a kind of routine, you know? It would be hard to start working with someone new at this point."

Melissa felt a smile creeping onto her face, but she bit her lip and forced it away. She didn't need Will to see how thrilled she was that Aaron didn't want to give up working with her. It was a definite sign that she was making progress.

"Yeah, okay," Will said. "I guess I can see that."

"I promise I won't blow it like that again," Melissa told Aaron. "Now that I know exactly what O'Reilly's looking for, I can help you ace the rest of these essay tests and any other assignments she gives you too."

"Cool," Aaron said. "So when do you want to meet again?"

"Is she letting you revise this essay?" Melissa asked.

"I think so," Aaron said.

"Then how about this afternoon?" Melissa suggested.

"Sounds good," Aaron agreed. "I better get to gym class—I don't want to have to do extra laps for being late. See you later," he said to Will. "And thanks, Melissa—you're the best," he added as he turned and jogged away.

Alanna Feldman

Stress Shield Instructions: On this sheet, make a list of things you can do to manage your stress. Come up with as many ideas as possible. Then transfer your ideas to the open spaces in the shield drawing on the next page. Get creative. Use crayons or markers to make your shield colorful. You can even paste on pictures from magazines or draw your own to represent each activity. Then the next time you find yourself in a stressful situation, take out your shield and use it.

~~Call Conner~~
Dance
Listen to music
~~Hang out with Conner~~
Write in my journal
~~Hug Conner~~

I'll have to make another list. I can't put half of these on my shield. If anyone in A.A. ever saw it, they'd say I was depending way too much on Conner. That I was just replacing one addiction with another.

I know I'm being dumb. Sandra said I could do whatever I wanted with this stuff because no one ever has to see it—not even her. But somehow just writing Conner's name on the list makes me feel dishonest—like I'm breaking some kind of rule. It's like, as long as I don't put it in writing anywhere, I'm not doing anything wrong. And I'm _not_. Except for maybe lying to Sandra about it.

CHAPTER
Hunting and Gathering

Andy grabbed his change from the woman at the cash register and made his way to one of the back tables in the cafeteria. Tia, Elizabeth, Jessica, Jeff, and Evan were already seated, and they appeared to be having a pretty heated discussion.

"I never said that," he heard Jessica exclaim just before he set his tray down on the table, taking the chair between Tia and Jeff.

"Maybe not in so many words," Evan said, grinning. "But that's what you meant."

"It is not," Jessica insisted. "And we never actually dated either."

Evan shook his head, and everyone at the table—except Andy, who had no clue what was going on—started laughing.

"What's up?" Andy asked when the laughter had subsided.

Jeff nodded toward Evan and Jessica, who were sitting on the other side of the table. "They're having a little disagreement," he said with a grin. "Evan says that Jessica told him he was the best kisser she'd ever met, and Jessica insists he's lying."

"I never said anything even remotely close to that," Jessica told Andy, leaning across the table to make her point.

"Yes, she did," Evan countered. "And we did date," he added, turning toward Jessica.

"No, we didn't."

"Then what exactly would you call those nights when we got together—just the two of us—and went out?" Evan asked.

"I don't know," Jessica replied. "But Tia and I have also gotten together—just the two of us—and gone out. Does that mean I'm dating her now?"

"Oh, Jessica," Tia said, running around to the other side of the table to give Jessica a big hug. "I knew we couldn't keep it a secret much longer."

"You're such a freak," Jessica said as Tia returned to her seat.

"What I don't get," Andy said, "is why the two of you are even talking about what kind of kisser Evan is. You're both seeing other people now."

"It's his fault," Jessica said, hitching her thumb at Evan. "He brought it up."

"Only because you said I had a huge mouth," Evan returned. "I just wanted to make it clear that my mouth is fine, and obviously it is, or you never would have told me I was the best kisser you'd ever known."

At that, everyone except Jessica—who was practically yelling, "I never said that!"—started laughing all over again. But even she couldn't keep a straight face for long.

"You know what I'm thinking, Evan," Andy said when everyone had calmed down. "I'm thinking you need someone else to vouch for you." Then he turned toward Elizabeth. "Is there anyone else here that could attest to what a good kisser you are?"

"Don't even go there, Andy," Elizabeth warned him from Jeff's other side.

"Liz?" Jeff asked. "Do you have any light to shed on this topic?"

"Once—a long time ago—way before you and I got together," Elizabeth began, without even looking up from the chicken patty she was cutting, "Evan and I kissed. But it was so quick that I don't even feel qualified to comment," she added, causing everyone else around the table to chuckle.

Jeff put his arm around Elizabeth and pulled her close, kissing the top of her head. He obviously hadn't been bothered by Andy's quip, and for that matter, Jessica and Evan were taking everything in stride too.

Maybe Dave was right, Andy thought. Maybe his friends were mature enough to take a little ribbing without getting all bent out of shape. And if that was true, then he could definitely go for it at Sierra's open-mike night tomorrow.

Andy glanced around the table at his friends, who were still joking and laughing about Evan's mouth and whether or not he was a good kisser, and chuckled. How could he possibly *not* go for it when they were giving him such great material?

"Hey, Liss," Will called, jogging over to her locker.

Melissa turned toward him and stood on her toes to give him a quick kiss. "What's up?" she asked.

"I was just about to head to the *Tribune,* but I thought I'd see if you wanted to go out for dinner tomorrow night—my treat," Will said. Ever since Melissa had made that crack about him not having time to tutor Aaron because of the *Trib,* he'd been thinking things over. She'd been acting really strange lately—putting so much time into helping Aaron with his English grade—Will thought maybe it was because he wasn't spending enough time with her. She did tend to get irritated about stuff like that.

"I'd love to, but it will have to be late," she said, unloading books from her locker and stuffing them into her duffel bag. "Is that a problem?"

"I guess not," Will said. "How late?"

"Well, I'm tutoring Aaron after practice," Melissa started.

"I thought you were doing that today," Will said.

"I am," Melissa told him. "But we're going to meet tomorrow too. We have a lot of work to do."

"Jeez—how much time are you planning to put into this, Liss? You've been seeing more of Aaron lately than you have of me."

"That's not true," Melissa said, although Will was pretty sure it was. "Besides—you know I'm only doing this to help our friends. Aaron *and* Cherie, remember?"

"Yeah. I remember," Will said. But that didn't mean he had to like it. "So what time do you think you'll be done?"

"Probably by six-thirty or seven," Melissa said.

"Six-thirty or seven?" Will echoed. "You get out of cheering at four. How much time does it take to help Aaron study?"

"*Will*," Melissa said, widening her eyes and glancing around the hallway. "Keep your voice down." Will sighed and leaned up against the lockers, causing them to rattle. "First, I won't be out of practice until four-fifteen tomorrow, and then I have to shower. So Aaron and I probably won't get started until almost five. And second, as I already said, we have a lot of work to do."

113

Will rolled his eyes. He was tired of hearing about Aaron and his stupid English grade. Why had he ever even told Melissa that Aaron needed help?

"I'm serious, Will," Melissa went on. "I really blew it helping Aaron prep for that essay test. All he needed was a B-plus and he would have been all set. And he could have done it too if I hadn't rushed through our session on Sunday. Now we have to work twice as hard to get his grade up in time for him to play in the tournaments."

Will looked into Melissa's eyes. They were so fierce, so determined. He wanted to believe that she was really just trying to help Aaron, but there was something about the whole situation that just didn't sit well with him. He couldn't seem to get past the fact that Melissa had completely forgotten about O'Reilly's glance-and-grade system. How could she have, after all the times Will had complained about it? It wasn't like her to screw up details like that. Then again, if she was stressed out because Will was spending so much time at the *Tribune*, she might not have been thinking clearly. And she did say she had rushed through the study session with Aaron.

"Will? Now do you understand why I can't make dinner until after seven?" Melissa asked.

"Oh. Yeah," Will said. "Well, maybe we should just forget about it, then. By the time we get to the restaurant, it'll be eight, and I don't want to wait that long to eat."

"So how about if we meet for coffee and dessert instead?" Melissa asked. "I can just bring a sandwich or something for dinner and eat while Aaron and I are working. And then you and I can get together afterward."

Will nodded. "Yeah, that sounds good," he agreed. "Let's do that."

"Okay," Melissa said, leaning over to kiss him again. "I have to go to practice. I'll call you later, though," she said, rushing off down the hall. Will watched her go, wondering if he was crazy for feeling like there was something wrong.

It's nothing, he told himself. He and Melissa hadn't been spending a lot of time together lately, that was all. And maybe Melissa was a little upset at how busy he'd been with the *Trib.* But she'd made plans to go out with him tomorrow night, so obviously she wasn't too annoyed. And if she was upset with him, at least she was willing to get together and work at it.

So quit worrying, Will told himself. But for some reason, he was having trouble taking his own advice.

"These are nice," Andy said as he and Dave sat down with their coffees. They'd managed to snag two of the comfy armchairs near the window at the front of the café, and Andy was pretty psyched. It seemed like every other time he'd come in, someone was already sitting in them, but tonight they'd been free.

"Yeah, I'm really into gray lately," Dave agreed.

"Actually, I'd call it stone," Andy said. "And the detail on the woodwork lends an expensive feel," he added, affecting a snooty accent.

"Sheesh, you pick out one necktie and suddenly you're some kind of fashion guru," Dave joked.

"Speaking of ties," Andy said. "How was the banquet?"

"It was good," Dave said. "I had to stand up in front of everybody to get my award, but it was kind of fun."

"Yeah? Sounds cool," Andy said.

"It was," Dave agreed, taking a sip of his coffee. "And after I got the scholarship, my father actually hugged me."

"Wow," Andy said.

"Yeah. I think it's the first time he's put his arm around me since I told him I was gay," Dave said. "So, all in all, it was a pretty big night."

"That's great." Andy nodded. "I'm glad everything went well."

"How about you?" Dave asked. "What did you end up doing?"

Andy took a deep breath. "Well, as it turns out, I had a pretty exciting night too," he said. "First, I ate dinner with the 'rents, then I did my homework, and to top it all off, I watched a cheesy made-for-TV movie."

"Entertainment at its finest," Dave quipped. "What happened?"

"It was pretty good, actually," Andy said. "In the beginning this woman is being chased by some guy, when she falls in a ditch and loses consciousness. When she wakes up, she's in a hospital with this handsome doctor, but she can't remember anything about the night before—not even how she wound up in the ditch. So anyway, she ends up falling in love with the doctor and marrying him, but years later, her memory comes back, and she realizes *he* was the crazy guy who was chasing her that night, and he tries to kill her all over again."

"And did he get her?"

"I don't know. I fell asleep," Andy said. "But probably not. It was a made-for-TV movie."

"You're right. They always seem to have those happy endings, don't they?" Dave said. "I wonder why that is."

"Because they're always on Monday nights. No one wants a bad ending on a Monday," Andy said. "You have to save those for the weekend, when you've got an extra day to recover."

Dave chuckled and grinned at Andy. "You crack me up, you know it?" Andy shrugged. "So when are you going back to the comedy club?"

"Actually," Andy said, lowering his voice and leaning across the table, "I was thinking about going tomorrow night."

"That's awesome, Andy! Can I come?"

"Shhh!" Andy hushed him. He looked around House of Java to see if anyone he knew was working, but it looked okay. All he needed was for Evan or Jessica to find out. Between the two of them there wasn't a wealth of secret-keeping skill.

"What's wrong?" Dave asked.

"I just don't want anyone to know," Andy said. "I mean, I don't mind if you come, but I really don't want anyone else to show up. I'm still not sure exactly how they'd feel about being in my act."

"Are you kidding? They'd love it," Dave said.

Andy shifted in his seat. "Maybe," he said, "but I'm not sure. And besides, I'd rather wait to see if I'm any good before I invite a bunch of people."

"You're going to be awesome," Dave said. "I know you are."

"Thanks," Andy said. "But I'd still like to wait."

"Whatever you say," Dave told him, and Andy grinned. He knew Dave would understand. It would be cool to have his friends there and everything, but it just seemed like it would be better to wait and invite them another time. If things went well enough for there to be another time, of course.

Dave Niles

To: tee@swiftnet.com
From: dniles@cal.rr.com
Subject: Andy's big night

Hey, Tia—

FYI, Andy's planning to go to the open-mike night at Sierra's tomorrow. It starts around 8 p.m., and I think it would be great if you and some of Andy's other friends could make it.

Just so you know, he's not planning to invite anyone. He's kind of nervous about the whole thing, and he'd probably kill me if he knew I was e-mailing you. But I think it would be good for him to have some support, whether he realizes he needs it or not.

What do you think?

—Dave

TIA RAMIREZ

To: dniles@cal.rr.com
From: tee@swiftnet.com
Subject: re: Andy's big night

hey dave,
    thanks for the heads up and you're
right about andy, he gets all shy
about stuff like this, but if he's
half as good as he was in new york,
he'll kill (as they say in the biz)
and then he'll be glad his friends
are there to see him.
    i'll see who i can round up and
we'll meet you there around eight.
    thanks again,
                              tee

7
Caught in the Act

"See," Alanna said, pointing to the painting of the rowboat. "That's the one I was telling you about." She and Conner were sitting at the exact same table where she and Sandra had sat yesterday at Still Life with Coffee. Alanna had decided to bring him there after school because she knew he'd like the idea of a coffee place that exhibited local artwork.

"So that's the boat you want to crawl into," Conner said with a smirk.

Alanna laughed. "Do you want to crawl in with me?" she asked.

"Maybe I do," Conner said, leaning in to kiss her. Alanna was just about to close her eyes and let herself melt into him when from out of nowhere, Sandra walked by.

"Oh, no," Alanna muttered, freezing up. *I thought she said she never came in here,* Alanna thought. Even so, it had been stupid of her to bring

Conner to a place so near where Sandra worked. What had she been thinking?

"What's wrong?" Conner asked, but Alanna just cringed as Sandra sat down two tables away.

I should probably introduce the two of them, she thought. But she knew there was no way she could get the words "my boyfriend" out of her mouth in front of Sandra, which meant the whole thing would just be awkward. So instead she gave Sandra a quick wave and then turned around and tried to pretend none of it was really happening.

"Who is that?" Conner asked, nodding in Sandra's direction. "She looks kind of familiar."

Oh, great, Alanna thought. Conner probably recognized her from an A.A. meeting. And if he recognized her, there was a good chance she recognized him, which meant Alanna would be doubly busted. Not only would Sandra know she was dating someone, but she'd realize that he was an alcoholic too. Then she'd really think Alanna was a lost cause.

"Have I seen her somewhere before?" Conner asked.

"Maybe," Alanna admitted. "She's . . . my sponsor."

"Your *sponsor?*" Conner asked. "Since when?"

"Since yesterday."

"That was quick."

"Well, actually, I've had her name and number

for a while now," Alanna explained. "I just never called until Sunday, when I was so upset about my father."

"Oh," Conner said, nodding. "So . . . do you like her?"

"Yeah," Alanna said, fidgeting with her rings. "She's really nice."

"Then why are you so nervous?"

Alanna stopped twisting her silver-and-amethyst ring and looked up. "Is it that obvious?"

Conner glanced down at her hands. "You're wearing grooves in your fingers."

"Oh," Alanna said, setting both of her hands palms down on the table.

"So what's up?"

Alanna leaned back her head and stared up at the ceiling, clenching her jaw. She was going to have to tell him. "It's just," she started, looking down at the table again. "I feel kind of weird having her see me here."

"Why? It's not like we're in a bar."

"I know," Alanna said. "But I still can't help feeling like I'm doing something wrong."

"What's wrong with drinking coffee?" Conner asked.

"It's not the coffee," Alanna said. "It's . . . *us*." Conner narrowed his eyes. "I don't mean there's anything wrong with us," Alanna added quickly. "I just

123

mean . . . well, you know. I'm not sure if we're really supposed to be dating."

"Is this about that speaker the other night?" Conner asked.

"A little, maybe," Alanna admitted.

"Because A.A. doesn't have rules about dating, you know."

"Yeah, I know." Alanna moaned. "But Sandra's sponsor warned her about starting new relationships during her first year of being sober, and I kind of get the feeling that Sandra would feel the same way." *In fact, I already know she feels the same way,* Alanna thought.

"Maybe," Conner said, "but that doesn't mean you have to listen to her. If someone told me to dump you, I'd tell them to go to hell."

"But that's you," Alanna said. "You can do that kind of stuff. It's not as easy for me."

"Well, then come get me, and I'll tell her," Conner offered. Alanna smiled. It was sweet of him, but he just didn't understand. He was strong—he didn't need other people's approval the way she did. Plus he already had a sister and a mother he could talk to, not to mention friends like Tia who would do just about anything for him.

But Alanna didn't have any of that. She just had him. And maybe Sandra. And she wanted to keep them both.

*   *   *

"This is awesome, Melissa," Aaron said, taking a bite of the sub she'd brought for him. "Food, music—comfortable seats," he said, bouncing up and down on one of the gray cushioned chairs that surrounded the table.

Melissa had gotten permission from Mr. Nelson to use the conference room in the guidance office for their study session, and it was perfect. With the door closed and the blinds pulled, they had complete privacy. Plus there was a radio with a CD player, so she could impress Aaron with her newfound love of rap music. Thankfully she'd gotten the CD they were listening to at a resale shop, so she'd only had to waste eight dollars on it.

"I've got to tell you," Aaron said, chomping down on a corn chip. "This almost makes studying fun."

Melissa smiled. "That's the point," she said. "The more you enjoy what you're doing, the better you do it. That's why you're so amazing at basketball—because you enjoy it so much, right?"

Aaron blushed and stared down at his hands. "I wouldn't say I'm *amazing.*"

"I would," Melissa said. She waited patiently for him to look up and then held his gaze. "And I just want you to enjoy our study sessions so you can be amazing off the court too," she added with a playful

125

half smile. Aaron shifted in his chair and swallowed hard, but Melissa kept her eyes riveted on his until he finally blinked and looked away.

"Yeah, well, it must be working," he said. "My English grade is way better than it was before, and . . ." He glanced at Melissa, but he was still having a hard time keeping eye contact with her.

He wants to kiss me, Melissa thought. *I know he does.* She eased her chair out to adjust the volume on the radio, making sure that she positioned herself closer to Aaron when she pulled it back in. *There. Now he doesn't even have to lean over.*

"So," Aaron started, clearing his throat. "What do I need to do with this essay?"

I don't believe this, Melissa told herself. Here she was, decked out in sporty clothes, listening to Ludacris, snort laughing whenever she could fit it in, and practically sitting in his lap. What was it going to take?

"Um, let's see," she said, leaning over to look at the essay. They were so close, their shoulders were pressed together. "Well, like I said before, the writing is fine—we just need to throw in a few more terms."

"Which ones?" Aaron asked.

Melissa turned toward him, her lips slightly parted, giving him one more chance to lean in and go for it. But all Aaron seemed able to do was stare at her and breathe like he was making a prank phone call. *Forget it*, Melissa thought. *I'm not waiting anymore.*

She leaned in and closed her eyes, pressing her lips to his.

"Melissa!" Aaron cried, pushing her away. "What are you doing?"

"I thought—" Melissa started, but she couldn't find the words.

"Well, you thought wrong," Aaron said, pushing back his chair.

Again Melissa opened her mouth to speak, but no sound came out. All she could do was stare at him and blink, wondering where she had gone wrong. All the signs had been there—there was no way she could have misinterpreted them. So then why had Aaron pushed her away? Why would he pass on the chance to hook up with her after the way he'd been drooling over her all this time?

They sat silently, the awkwardness just hanging there between them, until Melissa couldn't stand it any longer. She stood up hurriedly, tipping her chair backward in the process, and stormed out of the room.

I can't believe that just happened, she thought, running down the hall. What a disaster. She threw open her locker and grabbed her things, heading for the door as quickly as possible. Whatever had gone wrong, it didn't matter right now. All that mattered was putting as much distance as she could between herself and Aaron Dallas—fast.

And he could keep that stupid Ludacris disc too. She'd never liked him anyway.

*   *   *

```
Othello: O the pernicious caitiff!
         How came you, Cassio, by that
         handkerchief
         That was my wife's?
```

Wow, Alanna thought. *That's one good thing about Shakespeare—he really knew how to insult people. But I wonder what a "caitiff" is.*

Alanna checked for a definition in the footnotes, but there wasn't one, so she made a mental note to check the dictionary in her dad's den the next time she went downstairs. *Pernicious caitiff. I wonder if I can work that one into my regular vocabulary.*

With that thought, she closed the book and set it on her nightstand. The fact that she was actually beginning to enjoy Shakespeare was a sure sign that she'd been reading way too much of it lately.

"Time for an e-mail break," she told herself, slipping into the wooden chair at her desk and scanning her in box to see if there were any new messages in bold type. "Aha," she said, spotting one. "But who's sbietche002@healthstat.com?"

Alanna stared at the name for a minute before it clicked. "Oh," she murmured. "S. Bietche—*Sandra*." She double clicked on the message to open it.

To: alannaf@swiftnet.com
From: sbietche002@healthstat.com
Subject: Yesterday

Hey, Alanna,
  Who was the cute guy? Things looked serious, but I don't remember you mentioning him the other day. Maybe you can fill me in tonight.
    See you later,
                    Sandra

Alanna read the e-mail over twice, sucking in her breath. Great. Fantastic. Super. Sandra had figured out that Conner was more than just a friend. *She must have seen him leaning in to kiss me,* Alanna thought. And if she had, then she definitely knew Alanna had lied to her about not having a boyfriend, which was probably why she had sent the e-mail—to give Alanna advance warning that she expected her to come clean at the meeting tonight.

But I can't, Alanna thought. Because as soon as

she did, she knew Sandra would start in on how important it was for her to be focusing on herself right now—not a relationship. And then she was sure to say something about how it would be so much smarter for Alanna to get her own life under control before she started dating. But what Alanna dreaded most was hearing Sandra say how disappointed she was that Alanna had lied to her.

I can't do it, Alanna told herself. *I can't go to the meeting.* Sure, Sandra would probably be even more disappointed in her for that, but Alanna couldn't face her. Not now. Not knowing all the things she was bound to say.

Maybe Conner could tell people to go to hell, but Alanna couldn't. At least not Sandra—she wanted Sandra to stick around. She wanted Sandra to be part of her support system, part of her life. Unfortunately, that possibility was looking more and more doubtful by the minute.

Alanna Feldman

All my life, I've wanted a big sister. Someone I could talk to about sex and boys and hairstyles all that stuff that I would never bring up with my parents. And I know it's stupid, but somehow when I met Sandra yesterday, I thought maybe I'd finally found one.

Okay, so I only spent like thirty minutes with her. But still, she was so smart and funny and cool. And really pretty too. Everything I always wanted my big sister to be. And somehow I knew right away that we could be really good friends.

But I blew it. I lied to her about Conner even though I knew I should have been up front about it. Now she probably thinks I'm a total loser—definitely not the kind of person she'd want to take on a day trip to San Francisco.

I probably I shouldn't be so upset about it. At least I still have Conner, and he's more important to me than anyone else in the world. But I can't help being sad. I guess it's just kind of hard to let go of something you've wanted your whole life.

CHAPTER 8

Too Close for Comfort

This is it, Melissa told herself, sliding onto a bench at Natasha's. She had convinced Will to meet somewhere other than House of Java for coffee and dessert, just to make sure they didn't run into Aaron. And now she was getting ready to tell Will all about the kiss, just to make sure he heard it from her first. And, of course, to make sure that he heard her version.

Of course, there was a possibility that Aaron wouldn't mention it to Will at all. But if he did, Will would totally freak out on her, and that wasn't a chance Melissa was willing to take. *Just remember, the best defense is a good offense,* she told herself.

"How's your brownie?" Will asked, piling a big piece of apple pie à la mode onto his fork.

"Good. How about the pie?" she asked.

"Just a minute—I'll tell you," Will said, shoving the entire forkful into his mouth. From the way his eyes lit up, Melissa could tell it was pretty good. "Mmmm." Will nodded. "It's great. Good call coming here. Their desserts are way better than HOJ's."

"Yeah," Melissa said. She took a sip of her coffee and steeled herself. This wasn't going to be easy, but she had to do it. "Unfortunately, the dessert wasn't my only reason for wanting to come here," she said.

"What do you mean?" Will asked, furrowing his brow. "What's up?"

Melissa took a deep breath and closed her eyes. "Something happened tonight that I need to tell you about, and I wanted to make sure we were in a place where we wouldn't run into . . . anyone we knew."

Will set down his fork and pushed his plate out of the way. "What are you talking about?" he asked, leaning his elbows on the table.

Melissa shook her head and stared down at her hands. "I don't want to make a big deal out of this, Will, but I think you should know." She paused to look up at him. "Aaron kissed me tonight while we were studying."

"He what?" Will asked, narrowing his eyes.

Melissa forced herself to swallow hard. "He kissed me," she repeated softly.

"Did you kiss him back?" Will snapped.

"Of course not!" Melissa said, gaping at him. "How could you even ask such a question?"

Will leaned back in the booth and folded his arms across his chest. "I don't believe this," he muttered, more like he was talking to himself than to Melissa. "How could he diss me like that? We're teammates."

Oh. My. God, Melissa thought. *That was Aaron's problem.* Suddenly it all made sense. It wasn't anything Melissa was doing wrong that was keeping Aaron from kissing her. It was his loyalty to Will! Why hadn't she figured it out before? She'd been watching football players buddy up for years. She knew all about guys and their stupid "code of honor."

"That's it," Will said, scooting to the side of the booth. "I'm going over to his house right now."

"For what?" Melissa demanded. "To beat him up?"

"No," Will barked, but Melissa knew that's what he was thinking. She also knew that if he went over to Aaron's house, Aaron would give Will *his* version of what had happened, and that was something Melissa didn't want Will to hear.

Will began to stand up, but Melissa leaned across the table and grabbed his wrist. "You can't go over there," she said.

"Why not?" Will asked.

"Because you're way too upset. And you're over-reacting to something that really isn't a big deal."

"Not a big deal? How can you say that?"

"Easy—it's true," Melissa said. Will rolled his eyes, but at least he was sitting down. "Look," Melissa went on. "It was just a kiss, and he stopped the second I pulled back. Plus he apologized up and down for it and promised it would never happen again."

"Well, yeah—because you rejected him," Will said.

"I don't think that's the only reason. I think he felt really bad about betraying you, because he wanted me to promise I wouldn't say anything to you about it."

"Oh, so he wanted to lie to me too, huh?"

Melissa sighed. "Don't be so impossible, Will. *No*, he didn't want to lie to you. He just didn't want to lose your friendship over some stupid two-second error in judgment."

"And you believe that?"

"Yes," Melissa said. Will shook his head. "Are you telling me you've never made a mistake you wish you could erase?" Melissa asked him. "Or kissed someone that maybe you shouldn't have kissed?"

Will shot her a sideways glance. It was a low blow, and they both knew it, but it did the trick. Will slumped back in the booth. "Fine. I won't go over to his house."

"And don't say anything to him in school tomorrow either. Please. Just let it go," Melissa told him. Will was clenching and unclenching his jaw, but finally he nodded. It was almost imperceptible, but it was enough. Melissa knew he'd keep his mouth shut, which meant that she was more or less safe.

Alanna glanced in Conner's kitchen window as she walked up the stairs, pleased to see him sitting at the table, reading. "Can I come in?" she called, knocking on the screen door.

"Alanna—hey," Conner said, walking over to greet her. She stood on her toes to give him a peck on the cheek, but he turned his head and glanced at the clock. "Aren't you going to be late?"

Shoot. Alanna forgot that she'd already told him about tonight's A.A. meeting. "I . . . decided not to go," she said. "I wasn't really feeling up to it, so I just figured I'd catch another one some other time."

"Does your group have another one this week?" Conner asked.

"I'm not sure," Alanna admitted. "But if they don't, maybe I can just tag along to one of yours."

"But I thought you wanted to go to separate meetings," Conner said, narrowing his eyes.

Alanna sighed. "Okay, so I'll catch mine next week. Why are you making such a big deal out of this?"

"I'm not," Conner said. "I'm just trying to figure out what's going on. You said you wanted to go to more meetings—"

"I'm not the one who wanted to go to more

meetings. That was your idea," Alanna corrected him.

"Fine. It was my idea. But you agreed with me."

Alanna rolled her eyes, but there was nothing she could say. She knew he was right.

"So why aren't you going?"

"I just wanted to see you," Alanna said. "What's so bad about that?"

"Nothing—except that you're skipping your meeting to do it."

"So?"

"So you shouldn't be."

"Why not? I've never really gotten anything out of them anyway," Alanna protested.

"What about your sponsor?" Conner asked. "I thought you—" He stopped suddenly, staring at Alanna, and she felt like she could practically see the gears turning in his head. "That's what this is about, isn't it?"

Alanna folded one arm across her chest and rubbed her forehead with her free hand.

"Alanna," Conner started, "you can't start skipping meetings just because you're afraid of what your sponsor might say about me."

"I'm not," Alanna said. Conner raised one eyebrow and stared at her. "Fine. So I skipped a meeting. It's not like my car's going to turn into a pumpkin and I'm going to suddenly start drinking again or anything. What's the big deal?"

"You need those meetings."

"I do not," Alanna said. "I can handle things just fine on my own."

"Oh, right. Like you did before you ended up in rehab?"

Alanna crossed her arms and bit her lip in an attempt to keep it from quivering. She hated fighting with Conner. Why did he have to make this into such a big issue?

"Sorry," Conner said. He put his arms around Alanna and pulled her close. "You know I didn't mean that. I'm just concerned."

"I know you are," Alanna whispered, "but everything is going to be okay." And when she rested her head against his chest, she actually believed that everything *was* okay. Or at least that it would be, if she could just find a way to keep both Sandra and Conner in her life.

"Hey—I've got an idea," Conner said, pulling away so that she could see his face clearly. "What about the Y? They have meetings Wednesdays and Thursdays."

Alanna widened her eyes. The YMCA. It was so obvious. Why hadn't she thought of it? She could go to meetings there without worrying about seeing Sandra, and that would buy her time to come up with a good explanation for having lied about

Conner. Plus the fact that she was still attending meetings—*without* her boyfriend—would help Sandra to see that she could be responsible. It might even make her realize that Conner wasn't a bad influence and that their relationship was a good thing. And of course there was the added bonus that attending meetings at the Y would keep Conner happy too. He'd be glad to see her working at staying sober, and he wouldn't be upset with her for skipping meetings.

"You're so awesome," she said, breathing a sigh of relief. If all went according to plan, she'd be able to keep both Conner *and* Sandra—thanks to Conner's brilliant plan.

Dave pulled open the door to the comedy club, holding it for Tia, Trent, Jessica, Jeremy, Elizabeth, and Jeff. As they filtered in, the audience let out a burst of laughter, and Tia turned back, raising her eyebrows.

"Someone's doing pretty well up there," she said, making her way past the line of people who were standing at the back.

Dave stood on his toes to look over at them. "Oh my God, it's Andy," he whisper-shouted to everyone else.

"No way," Jessica said, pushing through the

crowd to get a look. "It is!" she confirmed. "And there's an empty table over here," she added, motioning for the others to follow. They ducked down as they walked to avoid blocking the people behind them and also to keep from distracting Andy. Once they were all settled at their table, Dave was able to focus on Andy, who looked like he was having a ball.

"So anyway, like I said, I'm a senior—at *Sweet Valley High*. Can you believe that name?" Andy asked. There were a few chuckles, and some of the people in the audience even shook their heads as if they were engaged in a personal conversation with him. It was a good sign. Dave could see that they were all absorbed by what Andy was saying.

"*Sweet Valley*. I mean, come on—that's not a town. It's a spot on the Candyland game board. 'Ooh—don't get stuck in the Molasses Swamp, Billy!' 'Watch out for the Gumdrop Forest, Susie!' 'Oh, no, Mary's lost in Sweet Valley!'" The audience chuckled, and Tia turned to smile at Dave. She widened her eyes, and Dave nodded back at her. Andy was pretty good.

"Of course, that's kind of how I feel most days at school. You know—like I'm lost in Sweet Valley. But it's okay. I've been looking around, and most of my friends seem pretty much lost too—and some of

141

them even grew up in Sweet Valley. Like my friends Jessica and Elizabeth."

Dave watched as Tia reached for Jessica's arm to her left and Elizabeth's shoulder just in front of her and gave them both a squeeze. The girls all exchanged nervous looks, and Dave felt his stomach tighten. *Uh-oh,* he thought. *I hope bringing them here wasn't a mistake.*

"Now, Jessica and Elizabeth are identical twins, and if I didn't love them so much, I'd hate them. And so would you—they've got that California thing going on. You know—blond hair, blue eyes, thin, smart, full of energy, nice. It's enough to make you sick, really," Andy said, to the amusement of the crowd. And, Dave was pleased to see, to the amusement of his friends too. Even Jessica and Elizabeth seemed to be smiling.

"But it's strange," Andy continued, "because they look exactly alike, but they have completely different personalities. For instance, Elizabeth has let loose a little this year, but for the most part she's had steady boyfriends. I mean, she dated the *same guy* for three years. That's pretty rare in high school. Jessica, on the other hand . . . well, actually," Andy said, scratching his head, "I guess they're not all that different. Because from what I've heard, Jessica pretty much dated the same *football team* for three years—which is sort of like dating exclusively."

"Oh my God," Jessica gasped, while the rest of the table laughed. Then she turned to Jeremy. "I did *not* date the whole football team," she said.

"Just about," Elizabeth teased, causing Tia to giggle.

"Uh-uh," Jessica insisted. "Just a few of them. Over several years," she added, pressing her lips into a pout. For a second Dave was worried, but when Jeremy put his arm around Jessica and gave her a playful squeeze, Dave saw that she was actually smiling. And so was everyone else. *Then again, how could they not be?* Dave thought, straightening up in his seat and beaming at Andy. His delivery was perfect, and so was his timing. The audience was practically hanging on his every word.

"Of course, there's my friend Tia too. Also gorgeous, but she's only about this tall," Andy said, holding one hand just below his shoulder to illustrate her height. "Five-one, I think. Now, knowing that, you might think that I could take her in a fight." Andy closed his eyes and shook his head, causing the audience to laugh. "I wouldn't even thumb wrestle that girl," he went on, "and I'm not ashamed to admit it. Because her boyfriend is tough, macho, superstrong, and a football player; and he absolutely crumbles around her too." Andy took a deep breath and ran one hand through his curly red

143

hair. "Yeah, I don't know what she sees in that sissy," he said. "I'd never go out with him. Unless of course, he asked."

Trent glanced at Dave and grinned. "You better watch out," he joked. "If he starts making big money at this, I just might."

"Trent," Tia said, swatting him on the shoulder.

"Oh—sorry, honey," Trent said, making a show of folding his hands together in his lap and sitting up straight.

This is great, Dave thought. Andy was really in his element onstage—it was like he was born to do stand-up.

"Of course, I should tell you that I'm actually not available—I *do* have a boyfriend," Andy said, nodding as a few people applauded. "Thank you," he said. "And you know, now that I think about it, that might actually be the first time I've ever used that word—*boyfriend*—to describe him." He cocked his head and said it again. "Boyfriend. Boyfriend. *My* boyfriend," he said, furrowing his brow. "Hmmm. I kind of like it, but . . . I don't know. I think it makes me sound kind of gay." The audience roared—especially Andy's friends, who had all turned to look at Dave.

I'm not sure I like this, Dave thought, feeling the burn in his cheeks. He sank down in his seat, a little wary of the attention they were attracting. Already a few people from another table had turned around more than once, as if they had figured out that Dave and the others were the friends Andy kept talking about. And the way all the others were paired up—Tia and Trent, Jeff and Elizabeth, Jessica and Jeremy—it wouldn't take anyone long to figure out that Dave was the boyfriend.

"So anyway, my boyfriend is a really great guy. There's just one small problem: he's still got one foot in the closet. I mean, he's out to his family and close friends—all the people that matter. The thing is, well—he seems to think that no one else knows he's gay. Like if he hasn't personally taken them aside and told them, they're not going to figure it out. But . . . come on. He's cute, he's clean, his clothes are always color coordinated, his hair is perfect. He's a good dancer, and he looks like Brad Pitt, but he's *never* dated a girl. I mean, really—there are only two conclusions people could draw: either he's the original Ken doll, or he's gay. Not that I'm implying Ken is straight."

"Kenny!" Jessica squealed, turning around and grinning at Dave, but Dave didn't find it all that funny. He plastered a smile onto his face and tried not to look upset, but it was hard to keep up the facade when he felt like the entire club—including all Andy's friends—was laughing at him.

145

How could Andy have done that? *He knows what a private person I am,* Dave thought. Yeah, he had told Andy no one would mind being part of in his act, but this was hardly what he'd had in mind. He'd expected Andy to goof on his *friends*—not his boyfriend. And he'd certainly never expected Andy to out him to an entire roomful of strangers.

Alanna Feldman

To: alannaf@swiftnet.com
From: sbietche002@healthstat.com
Subject: Last night's meeting

Alanna,

Sorry you weren't able to make it to tonight's meeting—it was a good one. If you make it to the Thursday meeting, check in with Carole. I left a packet of stuff for you with her. Unfortunately, I won't be able to be there, but maybe we can get together and chat soon.

Take care,

Sandra

Get together and chat? I don't think so. At least not anytime soon. Maybe after I've gone to a few of those YMCA meetings. Like twenty. Or thirty. However many it takes to show Sandra that I _am_ focusing on myself and that dating Conner isn't getting in the way.

Finally Andy noticed the emcee coming onto the stage, but this time he wasn't there to haul Andy off. In fact, he'd let Andy go for nearly fifteen minutes— way longer than acts usually lasted at amateur nights.

"Ladies and gentlemen, how about a big round of applause for Mr. Andy Marsden," he called out, tucking his microphone under his arm and clapping along with everyone else.

Andy's heart soared. He looked out over the audience, thrilled by the sight of all those people clapping— for him. There were even a few whistles, and some people at a table in the back were standing up for him. Andy shielded his eyes from the lights and nearly fell over when he realized who they were.

Tia, Trent, Liz, Jeff, Jess, and a few others that he couldn't quite see. They'd all come down to see him, Andy realized, his smile growing even wider. But how had they known? *Dave*, Andy thought, scanning the back of the room. He must have told them. But where was he?

"Nice job, Andy," the emcee said, patting him on the back.

"Thanks," Andy replied, and then he stepped up to the microphone and said it again. "Thank you," he called, waving to the audience as he headed offstage.

When he got to the back of the room, his friends were instantly on him.

"You were awesome, Andy!" Tia said, giving him a big hug, and all the others were right behind her.

"Nice show," Trent said.

"Yeah, you were great," Elizabeth agreed.

"You mean, none of you were upset?" Andy asked.

"Why? Just because Jessica gets around?" Tia asked.

"I do not!" Jessica protested, slapping Tia on the shoulder. "But it was still funny," she added, smiling at Andy.

"Thanks, guys," Andy said, feeling like he was floating on air. What an incredible night. He'd gone up onstage and slayed the audience, and all his friends had been there to see it. Except . . . *where was Dave?*

Finally Andy spotted him. He'd been so busy hugging and shaking hands that he hadn't even noticed Dave, who was still seated at the table. "So what'd you think?" Andy asked, walking over to him.

"Everyone loved you," Dave said. "Congratulations."

Andy narrowed his eyes. "But what did *you* think?" he asked. Dave shrugged and stared off into space.

Obviously something was bugging him, but Andy didn't have a chance to ask him about it.

"Hey—we're thinking about going for ice cream," Tia said, throwing her arm around Andy's shoulders. "Can you join us, or are you too much of a celebrity to hang out with the little people?"

"Are you kidding? He needs to hang out with us now more than ever," Jessica started. "Where else is he going to find such great material?"

"You coming?" Andy said, turning back to Dave, who slowly rose from his chair.

"I don't know. I'm not feeling very well," Dave said as they headed for the parking lot. "I think I'm just going to call it a night."

Andy walked Dave to his car in silence. In the distance he could hear the rest of his friends still talking and laughing, ribbing each other about the things Andy had said. It was great to hear, but he couldn't enjoy it. Not until he figured out what was bothering Dave.

"What's going on?" Andy finally asked when they got to Dave's minivan. "Are you upset or something?"

Dave cocked his head. "Not at all," he said. "I love looking like an idiot in front of all your friends."

Andy drew back. "What are you talking about?"

"That whole boyfriend thing. And me not realizing that everyone knows I'm gay. How could you put

150

that into your routine? You know how private I am about my personal life. Did you really have to out me to the entire comedy club?"

"I didn't *out* you," Andy said. "No one knew *you* were my boyfriend."

"Your friends did, and now they think I'm a complete idiot."

"No, they don't," Andy insisted.

Dave shook his head. "I don't even want to talk about it, okay? Just . . . go get your ice cream."

"Dave," Andy pleaded, "come on. You're the one who told me it was fine to use my friends in my act."

"Yeah, well, I didn't know you were going to make me look like a jerk in front of them all," Dave shot back.

"Hey—I didn't invite them tonight. *You* did."

"Yeah, and it was a big mistake," Dave said, getting into his minivan.

"Come on, Dave—it's not a big deal. No one thinks anything bad about you. I barely even talked about you up there."

"Well, *barely* was enough," Dave said, slamming his door shut. And before Andy could say anything else, he was gone.

Unbelievable, Andy thought, his heart sinking into his stomach. The buoyant feeling of being on-stage was completely gone. All this time he'd been worried what his friends would think, and they didn't seem to care at all. But Dave, who'd been so supportive of the idea of using his friends in his comedy, wasn't speaking to him.

"Over here, Will," Matt called, nodding toward a table where a bunch of their friends were already sitting. But Will shook his head. He wasn't about to eat lunch with Aaron—not after what Melissa had told him last night. Instead he steered Matt and Josh to a separate table on the other side of the cafeteria.

"What's up?" Josh asked as they all set their trays down. "Why aren't we sitting over there? Sturges, Dallas, Gamble—we always sit with them."

"Not today," Will said, stabbing a fork into his mashed potatoes.

"Whoa, Will—something bugging you?" Matt asked.

"Not something. Some*one*," Will said, clenching his jaw. He saw Matt and Josh raising eyebrows at each other, but he knew they wouldn't ask. That's the way they were. They didn't beg him for information—unless it was about Erika Brooks or some other hot girl, of course. Instead they just waited, figuring that if he wanted to tell them, he would.

When it came to stuff other than girls, it was like they were still on the football field and Will was still their quarterback. They'd wait for his instructions, and then they'd ask questions, but they never initiated anything. They just followed his lead. The problem was, this time Will wanted them to ask. He'd been avoiding Aaron all day—he couldn't even look at the guy. And now, seeing him at lunch, at their regular table, joking around like nothing had happened, Will felt like he was going to explode.

"It's Aaron," Will said, nodding toward the other side of the cafeteria. Forget what he'd promised Melissa. He had to tell somebody what was going on or he was going to jam his fork straight through the table.

"Aaron Dallas?" Matt asked. "What'd he do?"

Will tightened his jaw. Just thinking about it made him want to hit something. "He kissed Melissa."

"No way!" Josh said. "When?"

"Last night, while she was tutoring him," Will said. Matt and Josh both turned and glared at Aaron's table.

"What did Melissa do?" Matt asked.

"She pulled away from him. And then she says he apologized and said it would never happen again and everything, but . . ." He shook his head. "I just can't believe a friend of mine would do that."

"A friend wouldn't," Josh said. "Only a lowlife, back-stabbing, bottom-feeder scum-puppy would."

Will sighed. "Yeah, but I thought Dallas was okay."

"Me too," Matt said. "I'm really surprised."

153

"So what are you going to do?" Josh asked. "You can't just let him get away with a stunt like that."

"I know," Will said, "but I'm not sure yet."

"Well, let us know when you are," Matt told him. "Because we're all over that, right, Josh?"

"Right," Josh agreed. "'Cause that's just wrong. A guy doesn't mess with his buddy's girlfriend. Everyone knows that."

Everyone except Aaron, Will thought. But soon enough, he was going know it all too well. Because regardless of what Will had told Melissa, he couldn't just let this go. Especially now that his friends knew about it.

"You should have seen him," Tia gushed. "He had the audience hooked. I'm telling you, that boy has a gift. He could read *Crime and Punishment* and make it sound funny."

"Yeah," Conner said as he and Tia headed for his car. "He's always been the comic relief."

"Mm-hmm," Tia agreed. "Even when we were kids. You *have* to come see him next time. I think he might do it again on Sunday—or maybe next week."

Conner nodded. "Maybe Alanna and I can stop in."

"Oh," Tia said.

Conner glanced sideways at her. "What do you mean, *'oh'?*" he asked, mocking her sullen tone.

"Nothing," Tia said. "I just didn't know comedy was Alanna's thing."

"Her *thing?*" Conner repeated.

"Yeah, you know. I just mean—I didn't think she was the kind of person who . . . Let's just drop it, okay?"

"I'd be happy to, if I knew what I was dropping," Conner said.

"Look—I'm not sure what I meant," Tia said. "I guess I just don't see Alanna sitting in a comedy club laughing it up with the rest of us, you know?"

"No. I don't know," Conner said, his voice flat. "Do you have a problem with my girlfriend?"

Tia rolled her eyes. "No—I don't have a problem with your girlfriend," she snapped.

"Then what is it?" Conner asked.

"Okay, look," Tia said, stopping and turning to face him. "I didn't want to say anything, but . . . I'm just not sure this relationship is the healthiest thing for you."

"Oh, really? And who are you? My therapist?"

Tia dropped her head back and moaned. "Don't get all upset with me," she told him. "You asked."

"Yeah, and I shouldn't be surprised either," Conner said. "She's not exactly cheerleader material."

"Hold it right there," Tia said. "I'm not going to stand here and let you insult me like that."

"No, but you'll stand there and insult my girl-friend," Conner shot back.

"All right," Tia said, taking a deep breath and lowering her voice a few notches. "Look. I'm not trying to insult Alanna. I don't even know her very well, and maybe that's why I'm a little uncomfortable with her. I'm sure she's a good person. If she weren't, you wouldn't like her so much. And obviously, who you decide to date is your decision." Conner folded his arms and shifted his weight to his other leg.

"I'm just concerned about you, Conner—the way a friend should be," Tia went on. "Don't forget, I've seen you hit rock bottom, and it wasn't pretty. I guess I just don't want to see you get hurt."

Conner exhaled sharply. He knew Tia meant well, but he was still a little miffed. Where did she get off, judging his girlfriend? Especially when she admitted herself that she didn't even know Alanna very well. "Fine," he said, walking toward his car again.

Tia fell in step with him. "So we're okay?"

"Yeah," Conner said, but he couldn't help noticing the irony of the situation. Here Tia was criticizing Alanna when really, they were a lot alike. Tia was getting all bent out of shape about what Alanna *might* do to him, and at the same time Alanna was driving herself crazy worrying about what her sponsor *might* say to her. They were more alike than Tia realized.

*   *   *

"I'll see you tomorrow," Melissa said, pecking Will on the cheek. "Call me."

"Right," Will said, kissing her one more time before she headed for cheering practice. *Finally this day is over,* he thought as he started packing up his bag. Now he could head to the *Trib* and bury himself in work so he wouldn't have to think about Aaron Dallas anymore.

"Will," a voice called. "You got a minute?"

Will groaned when he saw Aaron approaching. "Not for you," he said, continuing to shove books into his backpack.

"Look, man," Aaron persisted. "What you said about me—it's getting around school. Chris Gamble came up to me in photography and asked me what my problem was—going after your girlfriend."

"Yeah, well, I'd like to know the answer to that one too," Will sneered. "But I have better things to do with my time than listen to your lame excuses." He slammed his locker shut and clicked the combination lock shut, then started down the hall.

"Wait, Will—you've got it all wrong," Aaron said, grabbing his shoulder.

Will spun around and shook him off. "Get your hand off me," he growled.

"Really, man. You have to believe me," Aaron said. "I wouldn't do something like that—you know I wouldn't."

"So what are you saying—Melissa's lying to me?"

Aaron held up his palms. "I'm not trying to start anything, Will," he insisted. "I just think you ought to get your story straight before you start spreading rumors."

Will dropped his backpack on the floor and faced Aaron squarely. "Yeah? So what did I miss? Did you try to grope her too?"

"It wasn't like that, man. I know you're not going to believe me, but the truth is *Melissa* kissed *me*. I'm the one who stopped it."

Will scowled. "You expect me to believe that?"

"I don't expect anything, but I think you should know the truth," Aaron said. "Melissa's playing you, man."

"What's your problem?" Will snapped.

"My problem is that you're saying things about me that aren't true, and other people are starting to believe it," Aaron said.

"Well, maybe you should have thought about that before you made a move on my girlfriend," Will said.

"I didn't kiss her," Aaron persisted. "I swear."

Will gritted his teeth and scrutinized Aaron's face. For someone who was lying his head off, he was doing a pretty good job of maintaining eye contact. He wasn't even blinking. "Why should I believe you?" Will asked.

"Because I can prove it," Aaron said. Suddenly Will felt a knot tighten in his stomach. Aaron seemed pretty confident about what he was saying, which made Will begin to wonder if maybe there was some truth in it.

Melissa certainly had been acting kind of strange lately. Totally changing the way she dressed, screwing up that essay test, putting so much time in with Aaron. And then practically begging Will to keep the whole kiss incident quiet. That just wasn't like her. Normally, if someone did something to upset her, she wanted to make them pay for it. So why was she pleading with Will to back down?

Will looked Aaron in the eye, holding his gaze, but Aaron didn't look away. "Fine," Will said, swallowing hard. Pride didn't go down easy. "You say you can prove it?" he asked. Aaron nodded. "Go for it."

Will Simmons

I don't know what Aaron's got in mind, but I do know one thing. He better be wrong.

The Truth Comes Out

"All right," the A.A. facilitator said. "So we'll take a short break and come back here in five minutes."

Alanna stood up and stretched. She had to admit, so far the speaker had been pretty good. But when they came back from the break, she was snagging a seat in back. Being in front was horrible. She felt like everyone was staring at her, so she had to be perfectly still and pay attention at all times. In the back at least no one would know if she slumped down and closed her eyes for a few minutes.

She turned around and headed for the back of the gymnasium, surprised to see that there were about fifty people in attendance that night at the Y. That was the other thing about sitting in the front—she hadn't even noticed how many people had come in behind her or who they were, but they could all see her. *That's it*, she thought. *A quick bathroom break and then I'm coming back here and staking out a back-row chair*. If only she knew where the bathroom was.

Alanna headed for the refreshment table—someone had brought in juice and cookies. "Excuse me," she said, touching a cute, thirty-something guy on the wrist. "Do you know where the rest rooms are?"

He turned to answer her, but before he could say anything, a slender woman with black hair jumped in. "They're right around the—Alanna?" she said, when she'd turned around all the way.

"S-Sandra?" Alanna stammered. "What are you doing here? I thought you couldn't make the Thursday meeting."

"I said I couldn't make the local meeting," Sandra corrected her. "I always come here on Thursdays so Sean and I can attend together."

"Sean?"

"Oh, I'm sorry," Sandra said, grabbing the cute thirty-something by the hand. "Sean, this is Alanna. Alanna, this is my boyfriend, Sean."

"Boyfriend?" Alanna echoed. "You have a boyfriend?"

Sandra laughed. "Is that so hard to believe?"

"Oh—no," Alanna stammered. "It's just . . ."

"Glad to meet you," Sean said, extending his hand.

Alanna reached out and shook it. "You too," she agreed. So Sandra had a boyfriend—*and he was in A.A.* That had to be a good sign. How could Sandra come down on Alanna for dating when she was doing it too? *Well, maybe because she's been sober for at least five years longer than I have,* Alanna thought. But still, the fact that she was seeing someone had to help. Didn't it?

Andy knocked at the door, half expecting to see Dave peer through the curtain and then walk away, leaving him standing on the stoop. But after a minute he heard footsteps, and to his surprise Dave swung the door wide open.

"Andy," he said. "I was hoping you'd stop by." Dave's voice was slow and serious, and Andy was pretty sure he knew what was coming. He was about to get dumped.

"Look, before you say anything, I just want to apologize," Andy said.

"Andy, you—"

"No, let me finish," Andy interrupted. "This is important." Dave folded his arms and waited while Andy took a deep breath. "Okay. I crossed a line last night, and I'm really sorry," Andy continued. "I know how private you are about your personal life, and I never should have put that stuff in my act. I guess I just got really carried away, you know? I mean, everything was going so well, I just kind of forgot where the boundaries were."

"Andy, I—"

"I'm not done yet," Andy said. "I've been think-ing about it a lot—pretty much ever since you drove away last night. I haven't been able to get my mind off it, and I finally decided that I'm going to completely change my act—no more relationship stuff at all. And if that's not enough, I'll just quit doing stand-up altogether. Because you're way more important to me than getting up onstage, and I know you've made a lot of sacrifices for me. So I think maybe it's time I made one for you."

"Are you serious?" Dave asked.

"Absolutely," Andy replied. "Besides, if you were bothered by what I said last night, it's only a matter of time before I start upsetting my other friends too."

"Oh, no. Andy," Dave said quickly. "you were great. You can't worry about what other people think. And you can't censor yourself just because someone you know might get a little oversensitive."

"But—"

"No, now it's your turn to listen," Dave told him, waving his hands. "I've been doing a lot of thinking too. I overreacted last night. The stuff you said about me—it was true. That's probably why it was so funny."

"You thought I was funny?" Andy asked, brightening.

"You were hysterical," Dave said. "I just took it all way too personally, that's all. And you're right, you know. Everyone knows I'm gay. When my dad told

Evan's mom, she just laughed. She couldn't believe he was actually shocked by it. And I don't really think he was even completely surprised. I think he was just hoping he'd never have to find out. For real, I mean."

Andy nodded. "Yeah. How are things with your dad?"

"Getting better, I guess." Dave shrugged. "It's still awkward, but . . . he'll come to terms with it. Eventually. And so will I. In fact, I think hearing you make fun of it last night actually helped me a little."

"Really?" Andy asked.

"No. But it sounded good, didn't it?" Dave said, chuckling.

Andy laughed. "Yeah. It did." He gazed into Dave's bright green eyes and sighed. He really did look like Brad Pitt. "So are you sure you're okay with my routine?"

Dave nodded. "Yeah. I can handle it. Or at least, I'll try."

"Thanks," Andy said. "You're the best."

"I'm working at it," Dave said. "Oh, but Andy—just one thing, okay?"

"Anything."

"Don't invite my dad to see your act anytime soon. I'm not quite ready for that."

"That was a pretty good meeting," Sandra said as she walked Alanna to her car. "Didn't you think so?"

"Yeah," Alanna agreed. And it had been. Especially since Sandra hadn't mentioned anything about seeing her at the café with Conner. And if Alanna could just make it to her car, she might be able to avoid the subject for another week. Or two. Or three.

"I'm glad you came," Sandra said. "It gives us a chance to talk."

Five more steps, Alanna thought. She could almost reach out and touch her blue Saab now. "Yeah. Well, here's my car."

"Nice," Sandra said with a nod. "So—tell me about the guy I saw you with. Is he anyone special?"

Alanna's stomach fluttered, and she almost groaned out loud. Shoot. They'd made it to her car, but not soon enough. She'd known all along that she was going to have to have this conversation sooner or later, but she'd really been hoping for later.

"Um, actually . . . yeah. He's—" Alanna hesitated. "He's my . . . *boyfriend,*" she managed with only a slight wince.

"Boyfriend, huh?"

"I know, I'm sorry," Alanna said. "I should have told you about him right away—like when you asked me if I had anyone else I could talk to—but I didn't dare."

"You didn't *dare?*" Sandra asked, creasing her forehead.

"I know it sounds stupid . . . but I was afraid you'd

be upset with me. You know, because of all that stuff you said about focusing on myself and getting my life straightened out before I started dating? I didn't want you to know about Conner because I didn't want you to think that I'd already messed all that stuff up."

"Have you?" Sandra asked.

"*No*—not at all. Conner's amazing," Alanna said. "He's the best thing that's ever happened to me. In fact, he's probably the only reason I'm not passed out somewhere right now. And I don't want to give him up."

"Then you don't have to," Sandra said quietly.

Alanna paused for a moment. "I . . . I don't?"

"No," Sandra told her. "Of course not. Sometimes the first year of sobriety can be complicated by a relationship, but you can't always control these things. You get to make your own choices, Alanna. No one else can make them for you."

"But—" Alanna started. "Then . . . you mean—you don't think I'm screwing things up by dating so soon?"

"It doesn't matter what I think," Sandra said.

"It does to me."

Sandra looked Alanna in the eye. "Well, then, no. I don't think you're screwing things up."

"Really?" Alanna asked.

"Really," Sandra said. "But I don't think you're handling them very well either."

Alanna narrowed her eyes. "What do you mean?"

"Well, now that you've told me about Conner, I think I understand why you didn't say hello to me at Still Life the other day. *And* why you seemed so nervous when you saw me at the meeting tonight."

Alanna stared down at her feet and scuffed her toe against the pavement.

"I'm guessing that's why you skipped last night's meeting too," Sandra went on, "and why you haven't been returning any of my e-mails. What were you planning to do? Avoid me forever?"

"No," Alanna said, kicking at a pebble. "Just for a little while."

Sandra chuckled. "What? A week? Two?"

"I don't know," Alanna said with a shrug. "Maybe three?" She glanced up at Sandra and grinned, and they both laughed.

"Well, then I'm glad we ran into each other tonight. We've probably just saved you three weeks' worth of worrying."

"Yeah," Alanna agreed. "That's probably true." She let out a sigh. "I don't know what my problem is. I always get so worked up about stuff and make everything about ten thousand times worse than it really is."

"Everybody does that once in a while."

"Maybe. But I do it *all* the time," Alanna said. "Conner's constantly telling me to just calm down and not get so freaked out about things. In fact, he gave me the exact same advice that you did the other day about my father—you know, that I shouldn't take everything he says so personally."

"Ooh," Sandra said. "Cute *and* smart. He could be a keeper."

"He is." Alanna smiled.

"Good. Then maybe I'll get to meet him sometime."

"I'd like that," Alanna said. "And speaking of meeting him, I'd better get going. We're having coffee in town."

"Oh, yeah. I should probably get back inside and see what Sean's up to," Sandra said. "So I'll talk with you later?"

"Yeah." Alanna nodded. "And Sandra?"

"Mm-hmm?"

"Thanks."

Andy Marsden

I knew it. Dave's a Saint Bernard all the way.

CHAPTER 11
Revenge

Melissa opened her locker door after cheering practice, surprised to see that somebody had jammed a slip of paper through one of the vents. She snatched it out and unfolded it.

> Melissa—
> I've been thinking a lot about what happened yesterday, and I can't believe what a jerk I was. If you're willing to give me a second chance, meet me down by the soccer field at 5:30. I promise you won't be disappointed.
>
> —Aaron

The soccer field, Melissa thought, holding the note to her chest. That was a pretty private spot. You had to walk down a wooded trail just to get there, and at this time of day there wouldn't be anyone else in sight. *Aaron must be serious*, she told herself.

171

She pulled her watch off the top shelf of her locker and checked it. Four forty-five. Plenty of time to run back down to the locker room and grab a quick shower. After all, she didn't want to show up all sweaty. And wet hair could look really sexy if it was combed the right way.

Ha! she thought, grabbing her things and heading back toward the gym. *I should have known he'd come around. Lust always wins out over loyalty. That's why guys are so easy to manipulate.*

"She was really cool about it," Alanna said. "I mean, she did say that I hadn't handled the situation very well, but she was totally understanding."

"Good," Conner said, taking a sip of his coffee. He and Alanna had decided to meet up at House of Java after their A.A. meetings since they both got out at the same time. "I'm glad it worked out."

"Yeah, me too," Alanna agreed. "Sandra's so nice. I can't wait for you to meet her. And I just know it's going to be really great for me to have her to talk to. I mean, not that you don't give me great advice," she added quickly. "Because you do. It's just kind of nice to have someone else to vent to once in a while. You know, so I don't always have to dump everything on you. Because—"

Conner put his hand on top of hers and looked

directly into her eyes. "Alanna, stop worrying so much about what I think," he said.

Alanna rolled her eyes. "I just can't stop myself, can I?" she asked. "Boy, what is my problem? Why am I always so worried about what other people think?"

"Everybody is," Conner said.

"Well, I'm going to work on not worrying about that stuff anymore and concentrate on trusting my own choices."

"Yeah?" Conner said. "And what about us? Are we a good choice?"

Alanna smiled and nodded. "Definitely. I mean, I can see why that speaker was saying new relationships can be so hard when you're first getting sober. It can be really confusing, and it's really easy to lose yourself. But I think you were right. We're different, and just because her relationship was a bad thing, it doesn't mean ours is."

"Are you sure about that?" Conner asked.

"Absolutely," Alanna said. "In fact, after this past week I'm more sure of it than I've ever been before."

"Good," Conner said. He took another sip of his coffee and stared out the window. "Because I hated going to those meetings alone," he said.

Alanna chuckled. "Well, I'm glad this is working out for both of us."

*   *   *

"Aaron?" Melissa called, making her way down the last part of the trail. It was just starting to get dark, and without the lights on the soccer field it was hard to see very far ahead of her. "I got your note."

As she rounded the last corner and stepped into the clearing, she saw him, and he was even more gorgeous than usual. He had on a gray sweater with a dark blue stripe around the neck, which showed off his broad shoulders and strong chest perfectly. It was going to be nice to feel his arms around her and his lips pressed against hers. Maybe it was because Aaron seemed like he would be a great kisser or maybe it was just because she was finally getting her revenge, but whatever the reason, Melissa could feel a surge of excitement running through her veins.

She walked toward him, her wet hair hanging over her shoulders, and stopped, just inches away. "Hey," she said, putting her arms around his neck. "I'm glad you changed your mind." Then she moved in, tilting her head ever so slightly to the right and closing her eyes.

"We can't do this, Melissa," Aaron said, backing away.

"What?" Melissa snapped. Had he gone totally crazy? "What do you mean, we can't do this? You're the one who invited me down here."

"I know." Aaron shook his head. "But I can't go through with it. What about Will?"

Melissa huffed. "Will doesn't have to know," she said.

"But you told him all about last night," Aaron protested. "How do I know you're not going to tell him about this?"

"I only told him about last night because you pushed me away. I was upset. But now that you're ready to respond differently," she said, approaching him again, "well—I'm certainly not planning on telling him. Are you?"

"Actually, he already did," Will said, stepping out of the woods.

Melissa gasped. "Will—what are you doing here?"

"Getting the truth," Will snapped.

"Hey, Melissa—don't forget to put in a good word for me while you've got your tongue jammed down Aaron's throat," another voice said. Melissa glanced over Will's shoulder and stared, gaping. Cherie was there too.

"No," Melissa murmured to herself. "No." *This can't be happening.* But no matter how many times she blinked, the image in front of her stayed the same. There they were, Aaron, Cherie, and Will. And they were all pissed.

It wasn't exactly the perfect revenge Melissa had planned. In fact, things couldn't be much worse.

WILL SIMMONS

9:59 P.M.

I had really thought things were going to be different this time, but I should have known. Melissa hasn't changed at all. She's just as manipulative now as she always was — maybe even more.

CHERIE REESE

10:01 P.M.

Wow. Melissa's totally outdone herself this time. I never would have believed it if I hadn't seen it with my own eyes. And now I'm pretty sure I'm never going to forget it.

MELISSA FOX

10:59 P.M.

All I wanted was a little justice. For Cherie and Will to know how much it hurts to be betrayed by someone you trust. That's all. But now everything has completely backfired. I can't believe it. Aaron, Cherie, and Will were all working together to make me look bad. How could they do this to me?

Check out the **all-new**....

Sweet Valley Web site—

www.sweetvalley.com

New Features

Cool Prizes

The **ONLY** official Web site!

Hot Links

And much more!